Shane Brown was born in 1974 and lives in Norwich, UK. He received a doctorate in Film, Television and Media from the University of East Anglia in 2014.

He is the author of the horror novels *Welcome to Marlington*, *The Pied Piper*, and *The School Bell*, as well as *Ghost Stories for Christmas*, and the young adult novels *Breaking Point, Breaking Down*, and *A Ghost of a Chance*. Shane has also written books detailing the careers of Elvis Presley and Bobby Darin.

Follow the author on Twitter @shanebrown74.

Copyright © 2022, by Shane Brown

Front Cover:
La Pie by Claude Monet

By the same author:

Welcome to Marlington (novel)
The Pied Piper: A Norfolk Ghost Story (novel)
The School Bell: A Norfolk Ghost Story (novel)
The Successor (novel)
Ghost Stories for Christmas (short stories)
Breaking Point (young adult novel)
Breaking Down (young adult novel)
A Ghost of a Chance (young adult novel)
Emilia (young adult novella)

Queer Sexualities in Early Film: Cinema and Male-Male Intimacy
Reconsider Baby. Elvis Presley: A Listener's Guide
Bobby Darin: Directions. A Listener's Guide
Silent Voices: Vintage Interviews with Silent Film Personalities (editor)

THE FESTIVE SYMPHONY
A Ghost Story for Christmas

Shane Brown

CHAPTER ONE

It might be a little unfair of me, but I blame Clara for everything that happened. If it wasn't for her, none of the events in the following story would have occurred. Not occurred to *me*, that is. Somebody else would have come across the manuscripts eventually, of course, but perhaps things would have played out differently for them. Their decisions might have been different to my own. I guess we'll never know.

It all began when an invitation came through the post to attend the wedding of a friend from university that I hadn't seen in the three years since my master's degree. It's fair to say that I'm not the best person at keeping in contact with others, and, while I have social media accounts, I don't use them a great deal. All the constant notifications on my phone annoy me, and the whole thing takes up far too much time.

My first instinct was to decline the wedding

invitation. It all seemed a little too much effort, if I'm being totally honest. It meant travelling about a hundred miles across the country, paying to stay in a hotel, and, perhaps most off-putting, I would have to pretend that I was happy to be there. Parties, I should stress, are really *not* my thing, and I knew that I would struggle to get through the day.

And then, before I could send off a reply, Clara texted me. Clara was the one friend from university that I had kept in touch with – although mostly because she wouldn't allow me to drift away. Even if I didn't reply to her texts and emails, she would try again a couple of weeks later.

I should say at this point that Clara had my best interests at heart. There was never any doubt about that. The only reason she bugged me in that way was because she knew I could retreat totally into my shell, and that doing so wasn't good for me. I had done that during the second year of my undergraduate degree, and it had resulted in a kind of breakdown and the drinking of lots of alcohol. It was Clara that had literally dragged me to the doctors, and I wonder what would have happened had she not done so at that particular point in my life. Maybe I wouldn't even still be here. I'd certainly had thoughts of suicide around that time, and I couldn't even really tell you why. Life wasn't bad, and I was rather enjoying university up until that day when I went into my bedroom in our student house and stayed there, coming out to grab some food, steal some alcohol from the other flatmates, and use the bathroom. Clara was so worried about me that, one day while I was in the shower (not a particularly common occurrence at that point), she went into my bedroom and took the bolt off my door. I swore at her a great deal for doing that, but thanked her later. It was about a week after that when she dragged me out of bed and told me I had an appointment with the doctor on campus. In the weeks that followed, and with appropriate meds, things got better, although I had had minor relapses since.

Clara's text had arrived a couple of days after the wedding invitation, and she suggested that I stay with her and her girlfriend for the weekend of the wedding, as they only lived a few miles away. It would be nice for the old university crew to meet up again, she had said, and it would give me a weekend away. I knew from that moment that I would end up going to the wedding, whether I liked it or not. Clara never takes no for an answer when she asks you if you want to do something.

And so it was that I found myself at the wedding on the outskirts of Marlington. It was far less stressful than I thought it would be. It was a relaxed and quiet affair, for which I was thankful, and no wedding supper as such. Just a buffet, which meant I didn't feel as if I had to eat lots if I didn't want to. Both the bride and groom had studied music, as Clara and I had, although they had gone down the jazz route while I had concentrated on classical. I shouldn't have been surprised, therefore, when I found out that the music at the reception was being provided by a jazz quartet instead of a wedding singer belting out *Proud Mary* and *Mustang Sally*. That helped matters, too, as did being seated beside Clara and her girlfriend for the evening. And I won't deny that it was nice to see my friends and housemates from university again. The catch-up was pleasant, and I was pleased that I had decided to attend, and knew that I had Clara to thank for that.

At midnight, the reception came to an end, goodbyes were said and hugs were given, along with promises that we wouldn't leave it so long before we all met up again. We all knew that those promises wouldn't be kept, even at the very moment we were making them. Life isn't like that. Once you stop seeing people on a regular basis, you tend to drift away from them, even if you don't want to. It's just the way it is, unfortunately.

Clara and her partner, Megan, took me back to their flat and we sat down in their lounge and chatted for a while before Megan excused herself and went to bed. I had a very strange feeling that this was pre-planned, and that Clara wanted to talk to me about something.

"Another drink, Jonathan?" she asked me, once Megan had left the room.

I didn't tend to drink alcohol, as a rule. I had got too much of a liking for it during my depressed phase at university, and so rarely drank afterwards. I wasn't tee-total, but I would certainly never keep any in the house. It would be too tempting for me, and I didn't buy any in case of visitors as I rarely had them. However, I'd had a couple of drinks at the wedding reception, just to chill me out a bit, and I thought that having one more at Clara's wouldn't hurt. She got up and poured us both a glass of wine, handed me mine, and then sat down next to me on the sofa. I knew that she was about to start "the chat" that she had probably had planned since she had sent me that text after I received the wedding invitation.

"So, what are you going to do?" she asked me.

"Do? About that?"

"Your life, silly. You're stuck in the middle of nowhere, working at some poxy insurance firm. I'm guessing there's no man in your life, and you probably haven't had one night out in a year."

That was Clara to a T. Always coming out with exactly what she meant, and not bothering to sugar coat it.

"That's not what you want to be doing, is it?" she asked.

In all honesty, I hadn't really asked myself the question of what I wanted to be doing. I was quite happy to plod along with life, and didn't feel the need to ask myself if it was what I wanted. I'm not the ambitious type, so I didn't care what kind of job I had as long as it paid the bills. All I needed was a roof over my head and a little money in the bank for security. That was what I told myself, anyway.

"I don't know what I want to do," I said. "I think I'm happy as I am, if truth be told."

Clara took a sip of her wine.

"You don't *seem* very happy."

"Don't I?"

Clara shook her head.

"No," she said.

"Then what do I seem?"

"Bored. Lost. Depressed."

I didn't reply. I was, of course, all of those things to one degree or another. If I didn't have ambitions or a hobby outside of work, then it probably *was* to do with the depression rearing its ugly head again, even if it wasn't otherwise an issue. The problem was that I had become so used to it lurking in the background that it was almost comforting.

"You're like you were in the second year of uni," Clara said. "And you remember how worried everyone was about you then."

"Clara, I promise you that I am *not* like I was at that point. I might not be making the most of my life, but I can assure you that I am, at least, functioning. You can see that for yourself."

"For now. But it's horrible knowing you're just going from one day to the next without any real purpose. You said you'd join a local orchestra or a choir, and you never did it. It would have given you an interest, and it would have…"

"…Given me the chance of making friends, and maybe even find a boyfriend. Yes, yes. I know all about that. But what if I don't want any of that? I don't *want* a boyfriend, Clara. I'm perfectly fine just as I am."

"You don't *want* a boyfriend? Or is it that you can't be bothered to have one?"

"Both!"

Clara finished off her glass of wine, and put the glass back on the coffee table in front of us.

"Why don't you come back to uni?" she asked.

"And do what?"

"A PhD."

That was the last thing that I felt I wanted to do. I had struggled to last the course during my master's degree. The fun of my first degree had gone, as had the camaraderie between us students. Most people doing a master's basically viewed it as an audition for a PhD. It was a case of trying to show this or that lecturer how wonderful your work was, and how committed you were to it. Then, if you were lucky, you might be viewed as a candidate for a PhD. Everyone pretended to be friendly with each other as before, but it all seemed so fake when people were actually competing with each other for the funding. I had found it rather unpleasant, even though I had had no intention of carrying on my studies afterwards anyway.

"I don't want to do any more studying, Clara," I said.

"You don't want to? Or is it just too much effort to relocate and leave that job you love so much?"

"I'm happy with what I'm doing."

"Admin in an insurance firm. Yes, you must be *so* happy. There's a funded PhD opportunity at the university, you know? I'm sure you could get it. There has hardly been any applicants and, from what I can gather, none of the ones they *have* had have been suitable. I reckon you'd be perfect for it."

"You reckon, do you? I think you getting me to this wedding was just a ploy, Clara."

I didn't know whether to be touched that she trying to look out for me, or to be angry because she was interfering in my life.

"You can think that if you want. I understand why you might think that way. But it's not true. I just knew it would be good for the university crew to take the opportunity to get back together."

"So you told me. And it was. Honestly. It's been a nice day. But, honestly, have *you* enjoyed your PhD?"

"Yes, for the most part. I'll be rather glad when the writing up is over now, but I think everyone feels that way after three years or more working solidly on one topic."

Clara seemed to be in the minority at having enjoyed her PhD. The others I had spoken to at the wedding had found it stressful, lonely, and were suffering from imposter syndrome.

"And what's next for you?" I asked.

"Academia, I hope. But it's a case of associate tutoring until a permanent position comes up. Jobs in arts and humanities departments are hardly plentiful right now. You know who to blame for that."

I did, and they were likely to remain in government for another couple of years.

THE FESTIVE SYMPHONY

"But just think, Jonathan," Clara went on, "a funded PhD gives you three years of guaranteed income, if nothing else. That's not to be sniffed at in this day and age. Unlike at your insurance company, you wouldn't be made redundant unexpectedly. Plus you could do some teaching at the same time after your first year. That brings in extra money, and you'd be great at it."

I knew that Clara was right in everything that she was saying, but was it something that I really wanted to do? I didn't think so.

"What's the project?" I asked.

"Alfred Taylor. His family donated all his papers to the university, and the project is to go through them and...I don't know...make something of them, I suppose."

Sir Alfred Taylor was a British composer whose works had always been overshadowed by those of his contemporary, Sir Edward Elgar. There was no real reason for this with regards to quality, but Elgar had made his name first, and Taylor was therefore always viewed as, perhaps, too heavily influenced by the more famous composer. That assessment was only partly true. Taylor's attempts at something more modern and progressive early in his career had been dismal failures with both critics and audiences, and had been forgotten pretty much ever since. Some composers find their work re-evaluated many years after their death, but that hadn't really happened with Taylor, although his pieces were still played from time to time.

He had a long association with the University of Marlington, having been head of the music department for the last twenty years of his life, and the university's reputation of excellence in the arts still remained, some eighty years after his death.

Clara had got my interest, and she knew it.

"What kind of papers?" I asked her.

"Diaries, correspondence, manuscripts, notebooks. That kind of thing. They're all kept in the library at the moment, albeit behind locked doors.

"Why locked doors?"

"I don't know," Clara said. "I guess they're valuable. Irreplaceable, at least. Or maybe the family put a condition on who could see them when they donated them."

"Maybe."

"You know you'd be a perfect fit for that kind of project."

An hour later, I was in bed in Clara's spare room. I hadn't expected to be interested in the PhD project, no matter what it was. But, for some reason, the idea of going through Taylor's papers and manuscripts intrigued me. Perhaps it was the fact that only I would get to see them – in the short term, at least. Or maybe it was because I rather liked what I had heard of Taylor's work. The association with the university meant that various pieces by the composer often turned up in concerts in Marlington, particularly those given by the university orchestra, and I had played in plenty of those during my student years. I had even played the solo part in a short concerto for violin and orchestra that Taylor had written. It was no masterwork, but the piece was interesting all the same, and deserved to be better known.

Taylor was best known now for a quartet of symphonic poems influenced by literary works: *Moll Flanders*, *Tess of the D'Urbervilles*, *The Fall of the House of Usher*, and *Edwin Drood*. They had been successful when first performed, and were still even played occasionally outside of Marlington, including the Proms from time to time. Virtually everything else had slipped into obscurity – not that this was uncommon. I'd fallen in love with the music of Arnold Bax when I was a teenager, but little of his work is widely known, unfortunately, although there have been some notable recordings in recent years – but they haven't resulted in a Bax revival.

I kept going over all of these things in my head. It didn't take long for me to get the idea into my head that I could possibly help create a revival of Taylor's work through the PhD, and maybe writing a biography afterwards. Perhaps there would even be some lost works among the manuscripts. I liked the idea of being responsible for a premiere performance of a piece by Taylor. It seemed mightily ambitious to think in those terms before even applying to take on the research, but the idea seemed very appealing. And would it really be so bad to give up my dull office job and move back to the city where I went to university? Marlington was a good place to live, after all, and I had little family, no partner, and only a couple of friends from work. I wouldn't be leaving much behind.

It was with these thoughts whirring around in my mind that I finally drifted off to sleep, and, when I awoke the following morning, my mind was made up.

CHAPTER TWO

I ended up staying an extra night with Clara, so that I could go to the university campus and see about the PhD project. It didn't take me long to realise that there had been virtually no interest in it, despite it being fully-funded research. I wasn't all that surprised. Taylor was neither well respected or well known outside of Marlington itself. Things progressed quickly and, by the end of the month, I was notified that I had been successful – not that there had been a great deal of doubt in my mind that I would be.

When I started work on the project that September, I quickly found out that the "Taylor Collection" was box after box of material, all of it totally unsorted, and in no order whatsoever. I realised that, before I could do any actual research, I would need to sort the material and catalogue it, if only for my own reference in the first instance. That was going to take weeks – maybe even months – of being couped up in a small room in the basement of the university library. Many people would have hated the thought of that but, in many respects, it was just what I was hoping for. There was little chance of being interrupted, and no need for me to mix with other people at the university. I was perfectly happy with that. I could shut myself off from everything, listen to music through my headphones, and throw myself into my work.

There was the occasional meeting with my supervisor, of course. I had been taught by Frank Clayton during both my undergrad and master's degrees, and we had got on well, and I liked his no-nonsense, tell-it-like-it-is approach. I was beyond pleased that he would be supervising my work. It meant that, for the most part, I would be allowed to proceed without much interference, beyond a cup of coffee together every few weeks to discuss progress and, eventually, the areas upon which my final thesis would concentrate. But that was still a long way off.

I had found a small flat to rent within walking distance of the university, and which I could afford without the need for a flatmate. There was no way I could cope with living with others, beyond the possibility of maybe getting a cat – but a cat generally didn't hog the bathroom, or cook and then fail to wash up afterwards. Having worked for a few years, there was some money in the bank (not a huge amount, but it was, at least, *something*), and the funding for the

PhD would be enough to live on. My social life was non-existent, and I didn't expect that to change. With no need to use public transport to get onto campus, my expenses were kept to a minimum.

Everything seemed as if it had worked out perfectly, and I was (at that point) thankful to Clara for pushing me to apply to do the research.

The first few weeks in the room at the library were difficult, though. I was confronted with the two dozen or more boxes of papers in the collection, and I had to work out how best to sort them. Would it be best to put them in date order? Or should they be organised by type? I started off trying it one way, and then gave up and tried another. It wasn't even as if each box only contained one type of document. The manuscripts, letters, diaries, and so on, were all mixed up together. Eventually, though, I found a way of dealing with the mass of material. It was very tempting to start reading the documents that I pulled out of each box, just to get an idea of what they were about (plus it was more interesting than sorting), but that was taking up too much time, and so I tried my best to stick to the sorting exercise first. I arranged to move some extra tables into the room – although there wasn't much space – so that I could put scores and manuscripts on one, diaries on another, and letters and other correspondence on the third.

Finally, after a month or so of work, I felt that I had made enough progress to meet with Frank for the first time.

"How's it going in there?" Frank asked me. "I'm sure we could find you a bigger room somewhere if it would help. Or at least a room with some windows. It must be horrible stuck in there all day."

"It's fine, really," I said. "I'm listening to music all day, and rather enjoying myself, to be honest. I haven't listened to this much music in years. I've finally found the point of streaming services."

I might have found a use for them, but I still didn't like them. I much preferred to collect vinyl and CDs, and I was rather proud of my collection, even if I sometimes wished I had someone to enjoy it with. I was perfectly happy with my single life, except in that regard. I wondered if, perhaps, I should join a music society somewhere, so that I could discuss the music I loved. Perhaps there was even one at the university.

"What's actually in those boxes?" Frank asked me. "Is there any rhyme or reason as to what is in there?"

I shook my head.

"None whatsoever. It's like three or four people were clearing out a house and dumped whatever they found into a single box until it was full, and then just moved on to the next. Heaven knows where they stored all of this before they gave it to the university."

"I'm surprised that they donated it at all," Frank said. "I've met the current generations of Taylors, and they are a secretive bunch. They haven't done much to keep poor Sir Alfred's name alive, beyond the ongoing grant for the university's opera production each year – although I'm sure they were happy to have the royalty cheques for his works until they went out of copyright ten years ago."

"Was it because he was gay, do you think?" I asked. "I haven't read much, but some of those letters appear to be quite…interesting. Most I've found are to Bernard Wakelin, but there are some predating their relationship."

While Alfred Taylor had been head of the music department in the interwar years, Bernard Wakelin had been head of the drama department. They had combined forces at work, and had a personal relationship of fifteen years or so as they entered old age. It was something of a secret at the time, but it became public knowledge in the 1960s, when Wakelin's memoirs were published, some twenty years after his death.

"I don't think it's anything to do with that," Frank said. "It's just the way they are, I assume. Some families are like that."

CHAPTER THREE

It was towards the end of November before I had completed sorting the documents into the various types, having got diverted along the way with some background reading, too, to vary my days a little bit.

Confronting me now when I walked into the little room in the library were three tables. The first was piled high with diaries and journals that were relatively easy to put into some sensible order. The second table had three separate piles: one of letters, one of telegrams and other communications of that nature, and one of cuttings from newspapers regarding the composer. Finally, there was a table covered in manuscripts and scores of Taylor's musical compositions. This table was, I thought, the most important, and needed to be sorted first.

I assumed that there would be some lost and unheard works among them, and I was thinking that the university orchestra and choir might be able to give the first performances of them at some time in the future. That was something that would bring Taylor's name back into the public eye, and might even lead to a re-evaluation of his work – and, possibly, recordings of newly-found works. I confess I liked the idea of being the one behind any such new awareness of Taylor's compositions.

It was clear that Sir Alfred was quite meticulous about how his work was presented. The score for each composition was dated in the top right-hand corner – the start date of the composition first, with the completion date underneath. And each page of manuscript had the name of the work written at the top – which was very useful from my own point of view, given how the papers had been dumped into the boxes, and how that had caused some pages of scores to get detached from the rest. My plan was to put the scores into date order as best I could, but I took my time over it, typing up a short description of each piece on my laptop as I came across it.

One of the first unknown works that I found was a short piano sonata dated 1881 – when Taylor had been just nine years old. I looked through the work with interest, surprised by how accomplished certain parts of it were – and how difficult. Many composers were known as virtuosos on their chosen instruments, but Taylor didn't fall into this category – or, at least, not as far as I was aware. I wondered how he could have written such a piece at nine years old if, in all likelihood, he couldn't actually play it. Some of the development section in the first movement was a little rudimentary, but the slow movement was truly beautiful, and yet remarkably simple. The main theme could quite easily have come from an English folk song – and I wondered if that *was* the actual source. I was no expert on folk music, but thought it should be easy to find out, although I was well aware that Taylor wasn't well known for using folk songs in his work – unlike someone like Ralph Vaughan-Williams, for example. I had an electric piano at my flat, and so I photographed each page of the sonata, in the hope that I might find the time to play it during the next few days.

I needed to speak to Frank about the possibility of taking some of the materials out of the library. I hadn't minded being couped up in the small room up until that point, but it wasn't somewhere that I wanted to spend three years. Besides, it would help me if I could go through the scores at a piano. I made a note on my phone to ask Frank at our next meeting.

The next manuscripts in the pile were song settings of poems by Christina Rosetti. These were from just before the First World War, by which point Taylor was already overshadowed by Elgar. I remembered having heard recordings of these at some point, but seeing the notation in front of me in Taylor's own hand, I was struck at how accomplished the songs were. Also noteworthy was how clear and organised his writing was. They *were* unmistakeably in Taylor's own hand – nobody else had copied them out – and yet there were no mistakes, no crossings out, unlike autograph scores by other composers that I had seen. It was quietly impressive.

It was late morning by this point, and I thought it would be a good point to break for lunch, but I was rather intrigued by a large brown envelope that was now at the top of the pile of unsorted manuscripts. It was sealed – with wax, no less. The front of the envelope had the word "symphony" written across it in large letters, with the year "1914" underneath. I knew that Taylor had written three symphonies, one in 1908 another in 1912, and a third, known as *The Marlington*, during the late 1920s. I remembered having seen the scores for those briefly when I had first started sorting out the boxes. Unless it was a revision of one of the earlier symphonies, this had to be a new work. But why was it in a sealed envelope when none of the other manuscripts were? Whatever the reason, I was rather excited at the thought of what could well be my first major find. There was no other information on the envelope, and so the only thing for me to do was to break the seal and look inside.

My hands were shaking as I picked up the envelope and broke the seal. As I did so, the light in the small room flickered on and off. Gale force winds had been forecast, and so I merely assumed that they had arrived, although there was no real way of knowing without leaving the room as there were no windows. I pulled my phone out of my trouser pocket and placed it on the table in front of me, so that I had easy access to the torch on it if the lights failed completely.

I reached into the envelope, and pulled out the contents. There were four groups of papers, and I assumed (correctly) that there was one for each movement of the symphony. The first page of the first movement was headed with the words "Festive Symphony," and that confirmed that this was indeed an unknown composition. Even so, I checked my list of Taylor's work, just to make sure. It wasn't there. I could feel my hands start to tremble with excitement at the thought of how important the papers I was holding might be.

The piece was scored for full orchestra, and, as I turned the pages, I could see that the movement was in traditional sonata form, but that the two main melodic themes were actually lifted from Christmas carols: *I Saw Three Ships* and *Past Three o'Clock.* They were interwoven together with remarkable skill, and with a bold use of the orchestra that wasn't generally associated with Taylor. The use of traditional carols and songs in the piece was surprising, but not unheard of. Many composers have used folk music in a similar way. I had played in the university orchestra for a performance of Bruch's *Scottish Fantasy*, which does a similar thing.

I put the first movement down on the table, and started to look at the second. This was a slow movement, as one would expect from a symphony of the period, but this was scored just for strings, and took the melody of *God Rest Ye Merry Gentlemen*, slowing it down to an almost funereal pace, and then subjecting it to a series of ever-more intricate variations – the final one leading to a dramatic and lengthy fugue. Taylor was more inspired here than in any of his other compositions that I was aware of.

As I picked up the third movement, the door behind me rattled, as if it were locked and someone was trying to get in. I got up and opened it, to see if there was anyone there. I saw no-one, and, as with the flickering lights earlier, I put it down to the wind.

The score for the third movement both shocked and chilled me. Whereas all the other manuscripts in the collection had been written neatly, and mostly without any corrections, this one was almost totally scribbled over, and not just in a way to indicate that the composer was unhappy with what he had written, but that he wanted to obliterate it. The pencil that Taylor had used had literally ripped through the paper at one point, and there was a spot where it could be seen that the lead had broken. On the top of the first page, the title "3rd movement" had been scratched out, and, in its place were one-inch-high letters that read "WHAT HAVE I DONE???"

I stared down at the manuscript, not sure of what to make of it. This was, clearly, the reason why the *Festive Symphony* was an unknown work. Taylor's destruction of the third movement – and "destruction" was the word that came to mind – presumably meant that the composer had no intention of the piece ever being played. But why destroy the music in that way?

Even if he was unhappy with it, that would be no reason to do what he had done. It didn't make any sense – not yet, anyway – and I wasn't able to work out whether the scrawled words at the top of the score were a reference to the music itself, or the fact that it had all been scratched over by what appeared to be an angry (or was it frightened?) composer. In other words, were the words "what have I done" written before or after the movement was obliterated?

I looked at the rest of the pages of the third movement, and, as I suspected, they had all been treated in a similar fashion. Virtually nothing of the notation remained. On the third page, Taylor's pencil had missed eight bars of the first violin part, and I took a photo of it, intrigued as to whether it was enough for me to identify the main theme he had used in the movement. I also took pictures of the first page, intending to show it to Frank as soon as I could, to see what he would make of it.

I turned back to the page with a few bars of notation left untouched, and sang the bars to myself. The melody, such as it was, was not familiar to me. It certainly wasn't a Christmas tune that I had heard before, but it was an oddly haunting sequence of notes, almost mystical. Perhaps it was a folk tune of some kind, or maybe based on an obscure medieval hymn. My knowledge of that era was very narrow, and I wondered where Alfred Taylor had found the tune. The date on the first page of the movement was May 1914 – a few months later than the first two movements. I decided that I would dig out the diary for that year, in order to see if there were references to the piece in there. Surely, if Taylor had been driven to violently scrawl over what he had written, he would have mentioned it in a diary? Perhaps there was also something in his correspondence.

I pushed the papers away from me, suddenly realising that I wasn't feeling well. It had been late morning when I had pulled the symphony from its envelope, and I was surprised to see that it was now nearly four o'clock in the afternoon. No wonder why I was feeling a little strange. I had eaten nothing since breakfast, and not drunk anything in four or five hours. My head was beginning to throb, and I wondered if I might be getting a migraine – something that I suffered from quite regularly when I pushed myself too hard.

I decided that it would be best if I went home for the day and then come back tomorrow to find the diaries. I had a sudden urge to leave the room that I had been in all day. I just wanted to go home and try to forget about the symphony for the evening. I quickly got my things together, locked the door, and handed the key in at the archive desk.

"Having an early night?" Janice asked me from behind the desk.

Janice was the only person I ever had contact with in the library. She had been friendly to me ever since the start of my project, even bringing me a cup of tea some afternoons, and stopping to chat for ten minutes or so.

"Yes. I didn't break for lunch, and I'm feeling the worse for wear, to be honest. I just need a good meal, and maybe a doze."

She smiled at me.

"Well, you look after yourself, Jonathan. You are looking a little peaky, if you don't mind me saying."

"I feel it. I hope I'm not coming down with something."

I said goodbye to her, and went on my way, stopping to buy a bottle of water from the shop on campus before starting my journey home. The water made me feel a little better, but not much.

The weather had taken a turn for the worse while I had been hidden away in the windowless room in the library. High winds had been forecast, and they had certainly arrived, and, going by the clouds in the sky, rain would soon follow. If there had been a direct bus route to my house, I would have taken a bus that day, but I had no intention of going all the way into the city centre on one bus only to come all of the way back out again on another to get home. The wind was blowing in my face, and it made me feel even more tired, but I continued to battle against it as I walked. I had hoped to get home before the rain started, but I was still about five minutes away when the first drops fell from the sky. I hurried along, trying to avoid the worst, but, within seconds, it had turned into a downpour, and the wind blew the rain straight into my face. The mix of the rain with the strong winds made it difficult for me to breathe, and I wished that I had dressed more appropriately for what had been forecast. An umbrella would have been pointless, as it would have blown inside out within seconds, but I could have done with a scarf to cover my nose and mouth. I made a mental note to keep one in my rucksack for the rest of the autumn and winter.

By the time I arrived home, I was feeling both ill and weak – so weak, in fact, that I struggled to walk up the stairs to my flat when I saw that the lift was out of order. When I eventually got there, I went inside, closing the front door behind me, and leaning against it. Somehow, I had to summon the strength to get my soaked clothes off and, hopefully, get myself a hot drink. I kicked off my shoes, and looked down, dismayed, at my wet socks. I stumbled through into the kitchen and put on the kettle before making my way into my bedroom. I sat on the edge of the bed, and pulled off my socks, and dropped them onto the floor. I started to undo my shirt buttons, but it took longer than it should have done as my hands were shaking. Eventually, when I had the shirt half open, I just pulled it over my head. Once I had got out of my trousers, I realised that the rain had soaked through them to my boxer shorts, and so took those off, too. I sat there, naked, on the edge of the bed, trying to summon the strength to get up, but the room started to whirl around me, and I slumped back onto the bed, and the darkness came.

CHAPTER FOUR

I was sitting on the stage, playing in a concert performed by the university orchestra. It was the second time that I had played with them, and it was a Borodin symphony that took up the second half of the performance. All of the orchestra was playing the Borodin, but the music that I was playing was different. The music in front of me was the eight surviving bars of the destroyed third movement of the *Festive Symphony*. It was repeated on the sheet music over and over, but, as I played it, the audience members started walking out of the theatre, and the other players in the orchestra stopped what they were doing and just stared at me, blaming me for the diminishing audience numbers. The only sound now was my own violin, playing that eight-bar phrase continuously. Eventually, there was just one person left in the audience. I strained to see who it was, but my eyes couldn't focus. I had my reading glasses on, so that I could see the music in front of me. Anything beyond a few feet away was just a blur, but I could at least see that there was someone there. Or some*thing* there. Even as I dreamed, I asked myself why I would think that whoever was in the audience wasn't human. That made no sense. Eventually, the last audience member got up from their seat and started walking down the steps towards the stage, and, at the same time, the rest of the orchestra started to rush off stage. And then, the figure was directly in front of me.

I woke up on the bed, and looked around me, panicking. It took a few seconds for me to realise where I was, and that I had been dreaming. I was soaked in sweat, but also freezing cold – no doubt because it was getting towards the backend of November and I had gone to sleep naked on the bed and with no covers over me. My head was still pounding – far worse than any of the hangovers I had suffered during my drinking phase at university.

I wasn't sure what was wrong with me, but knew that it wasn't good. I had an urge to shower off the sweat that I was covered in, and hoped that it would help wake me up and make me focus. My trousers were still on the floor, and I reached down and took my mobile phone from the pocket. It was nine o'clock. I'd been asleep for more than three hours. I slowly manoeuvred myself so that I was sitting on the edge of the bed, and then slowly stood up. The room around me seemed to be spinning, but I tried to steady myself, and the room slowed down. My throat was dry, and I went into the bathroom and drank some water straight from the tap. Then, I turned on the shower and sat down on the closed toilet seat, waiting for the water to get hot.

I only managed a couple of minutes under the running water. I felt disoriented and dizzy, and I was afraid that I might fall over. Wrapping a towel around my waist, I went down the hallway to the kitchen and made myself a cup of tea. I was hungry, but had no inclination to eat. I grabbed a pack of biscuits from the cupboard and took them and the tea back to my bedroom. I put them down on the bedside table and climbed into bed.

I stayed there for virtually the entirety of three days, only getting out of bed to get a drink or use the toilet. I tried to sleep through whatever was ailing me, but a hacking cough kept me awake. On the second or third day (I don't remember which), I found a Covid test kit in the kitchen drawer and used it, but it was negative. Whatever I had caught on campus, it wasn't the dreaded virus, which I guessed could only be good news.

On the fourth day, I woke up and realised that my pounding headache had subsided, and the cough wasn't as bad as it was. Even better, I felt vaguely human again. The room had stopped spinning, and my stomach growled at me through hunger. The bed clothes smelled of sweat and that strangely recognisable odour of illness. I needed to freshen up to get rid of the same smell that was coming from me. After a shower, and pulling on some lounge pants and a long-sleeved T-shirt, I made myself some tea and toast, and went to sit down in the living room, switching on the television to catch up on the news.

After I'd eaten my toast, I opened the curtains that I couldn't remember closing, and looked out on the street below. Clearly, the wind and rain that I had walked home in a few days earlier had got worse, and then continued for a few days. Many of the trees across the street had lost some branches, and there was still water on the surface of the road. The news had reports of flooding in many parts of the country, including not far from where I was living, with the River Marl having broken its banks. There were benefits from living in a second-floor flat – not much risk of being flooded.

After an hour or so, I moved over to the table on which I had my laptop. I turned the machine on and then checked my emails. There were a couple from Frank, who was a little worried that he hadn't heard from me, and I hadn't been seen on campus. Frank had known me during my period of mental health issues while I was doing my undergrad degree and was probably worried that something similar had occurred again. I sent him an email to say that I had merely been unwell – although I didn't tell him *how* unwell. I told him that I'd take a few days to get better and then be along to see him. I wanted to tell him about the symphony that I'd found, but I was beginning to feel sleepy again, and so decided to tell him about that in person.

As I turned off the laptop, I realised that I could hear the sound of running water. I checked the kitchen sink first, and then went into the bathroom. It was one of those bathrooms where the electric shower is situated above the bath, so you could choose which of the two you wanted to use. I'd had a shower not long before, and knew that I hadn't used the bath in at least a month – probably longer. Despite this, the plug was in the bath, and the bath taps were on, with the water filling half of the bath. I knew that I hadn't turned the bath taps on while I was in there. I turned them off (and double-checked that they were tightly off) and took the plug out of the bath and watched as the water disappeared down the plughole.

I couldn't work out how the bath had been filled. Perhaps it was me, after all. Maybe I wasn't feeling as well as I thought, and was still a little bit out of it and had turned on the taps without meaning to. Despite knowing deep down that this wasn't the case, I tried to convince myself otherwise, as it was the only thing that made any sense.

I had been awake for a couple of hours by that point, and realised that was my limit for now. I went into the bedroom, determined to change the bed clothes before I went back to sleep, but all I managed was to strip off the bottom sheet and the quilt cover. I left them in a pile on the floor and climbed on to the bare mattress and pulled the quilt over me and went back to sleep.

CHAPTER FIVE

"A complete symphony? Really?"

It was a week later, and I was finally feeling better, and had arranged to meet Frank to tell him about my find.

"Yes," I said. "And it's not a youth work, either. Not something he wrote as a teenager and then hid away, a little embarrassed about it when he got older. And the main themes are from carols, and then he develops them just as he would if he had come up with them himself."

"So, why hasn't it been performed? Frank asked. "Why was it just filed away somewhere? That doesn't make much sense."

"Because of this."

I took my mobile phone from my pocket and showed Frank the pictures that I had taken of the manuscript more than a week earlier.

"This is the first movement," I said. "Perfectly normal. Neatly written, just like all of the manuscripts I've looked at."

"OK."

"Now take a look at the third movement."

I brought up the images of the scratched out score. Frank looked at it with raised eyebrows.

"He clearly took a disliking to that," he said, more than a little sarcastically. "Does the entire movement look like that?"

"Yeah. All but a few bars on a later page, which I think he missed by accident rather than design."

"What does that say at the top of the page?"

"It says, 'what have I done?'"

"What does that mean?"

I shrugged my shoulders.

"I don't know, in all honesty. I don't know whether he's writing that about the piece itself, or about what he has done to it. There's no way of knowing. I thought that, perhaps, the best thing for me to do is to follow this up before moving on to the rest of the scores in the collection. My plan is to try to find the correspondence from the period, and to see if the diaries and letters cover it, too."

Frank nodded.

"Yes, that seems like a sensible idea. If there are diaries from when this was composed, it seems unlikely that he would *not* have written about it given that it appears to be both a major work *and* something he clearly took a sudden dislike to. And you might as well follow it up now rather than later. If I were you, I'd be doing the same thing. Besides, it will make a change for you after going through those boxes and putting them in order for weeks."

That was certainly true.

I took the opportunity to ask Frank if I could take some of the documents home with me, but he was uncertain about the idea.

"I'd rather give you the code to the photocopier and ask you to make copies of what you want to look at. Just in case. It'll be a bit tedious, of course, but it won't take that long to photocopy a whole diary if you want to. Are you thinking of working from home?"

"Just over the next month," I said, "The university closes for ten days or so over Christmas, and I'm likely to get bored. I might as well use the time constructively. Besides, I'm still not feeling a hundred percent after whatever bug I had last week."

Frank nodded, and finished his coffee.

"Just remember this isn't a race. It doesn't have to be finished as quickly as you can. It's alright to take time off over Christmas."

But I didn't want to do that. I had got rather frustrated being halted in my work due to illness just as it had got more interesting, and I didn't want to put it aside again over the Christmas period, other than the few days when I would go home to see my parents.

After finishing my meeting with Frank, I made my way to one of the campus eateries for lunch, and then walked across to the library.

There was a different woman to usual behind the counter in the archives room, and I introduced myself to her before I went through to what I now viewed as *my* room.

"I was told you'd be coming a couple of days ago," the woman said.

"I was ill."

"You could have told me."

"I'm sorry. I didn't know that I had to."

"Janice is in hospital, in case you were wondering."

I hadn't been wondering; I'd just assumed she had a day off.

"I'm sorry," I said. "I hope she feels better soon."

"She fell down. Broke her hip."

"That's awful."

"She did it in here. On the last day you came in. She was locking the door to the room you had been using. You'd left it unlocked."

Had I? I might have been feeling unwell when I last left the Taylor room, but I was pretty sure I had locked it. I always tried the handle a couple of times to make sure that I had. Perhaps I had forgotten.

"I wasn't well last time I was here," I said. "I'm sorry if I left the door unlocked. It wasn't intentional."

"I never said it was, but it's a good job that she checked."

The conversation was going nowhere, and so I said that I had better be getting along, and went off to the room.

I thought about the poor librarian who had fallen

over just outside the door, and I felt strangely guilty. I told myself off for feeling that way. What had happened had not been my fault.

I tried to put it all out of my mind as I once again took the *Festive Symphony* from its envelope. As I did so, I realised that I hadn't got around to looking at the fourth and final movement, after being somewhat shocked by the state of the third one. I found it quickly, and was almost relieved that it was in the neat hand of the first two, and without any of the violent scribbling of the third. As with movements one and two, the main themes were taken from Christmas carols, in this case the *Coventry Carol* and *The Holly and the Ivy*. I didn't need to sing or play the score, for I recognised the tunes instantly – I had sung them many times in choirs.

As I put the fourth and final movement back on the table, I realised that its complete form meant that Taylor had *gone back* to the third movement and desecrated it later. But how much later, and why? I pulled those pages in front of me, and looked down at them.

What Have I Done?

"What do you mean by that, Alfred?" I said, quietly to myself, and then pulled the box of diaries towards me, trying to find the one for 1914 to see if it contained any clues as to what had happened.

CHAPTER SIX

The one thing that I hadn't done yet was play through the scores on a piano.

The electric piano at the flat was something that I hadn't yet assembled. The keyboard was still stored under the bed from when I first moved in, and the stand for it was tucked away in the built-in wardrobe. I had intended to put it together on the night that I had come home ill a couple of weeks earlier, but the virus that I'd had meant that I hadn't got around to it.

On the day that I had returned to the library, I decided I should finally put the thing together. I dug out my electric screwdriver and set about it as soon as I got home. I knew that, if I left it until after I'd eaten, I'd put it off again. In the end, it didn't take long, and, in half an hour or so, the piano was in place in a corner of the bedroom.

I switched it on and sat down, thinking it was

better to play it now rather than later in the evening, bearing in mind that the sound might be heard in other flats in the block, although I could use headphones if I needed to. I took my copy of the early Mozart sonatas from the book shelf, and opened it at a movement I knew that I could cope with. I might have been a very good violin player, but the same couldn't be said about my piano skills – and there was also the fact that I hadn't played at all in several months.

Having plonked rather hesitantly through the Mozart that I had learned as a teenager, I took out my mobile phone and turned to the photo that I had taken of the first page of the early piano sonata. In truth, the photo was too small to read it properly but, through leaning forward and squinting at it, I managed to get a rough idea of how it sounded.

I then swiped through the next photos until I got to the one of the few bars that were visible from the third movement of the *Festive Symphony*. I played the violin part, but it was no more familiar to me than when I had hummed my way through it in the room at the library. I decided that, the next day, I should photocopy the diary and take proper copies of the score of the symphony, too.

I got up from the piano and started to walk through to the living room, but, in the hallway, were a series of wet footprints. I stopped, looking down at them, and trying to work out where they had come from. I'd had a shower before I went on campus, but that was eight hours earlier, and so, even if I'd walked out of the bathroom without getting dry first, the footprints wouldn't still be there now. Besides, they didn't even come from the bathroom, but started halfway down the hall. Similarly, they lasted for five or six steps and then stopped just as abruptly. It was very strange, but I tried to shrug it off, telling myself that there was a logical explanation, and I just hadn't thought of it yet.

The next day, I spent much of the morning at the photocopier in the library, trying to take copies of the 1914 diary and the score of the symphony. Sadly, the machine seemed intent on jamming every few minutes, and, before long, my patience wore thin. I asked the rather snooty stand-in receptionist if there was another machine I could use.

"Is one not enough for you?" she asked.

With that, I walked away without even answering her. She wasn't worth the effort.

If nothing else, the photocopier got me out of the small room I had spent most of my time in. Something had happened since I had returned to campus after my illness. I had a strange feeling of darkness. I can't explain it any better than that. It was almost as if there was a huge weight pressing down on my head and shoulders. I almost expected to see it when I looked in the mirror. I knew, of course, that it wasn't a physical presence, and had a horrible feeling that it might be a more serious return of the depression that I had gone through during my first degree. Strangely, though, it made me feel hopeless rather than sad, as if I was aware of some impending tragedy, and could do nothing about it. Whatever the cause of it, it made me feel incredibly tired, and I wondered if, perhaps, I hadn't quite shrugged off my illness from a couple of weeks earlier as well as I thought. I hoped that it wasn't going to return. I was in no hurry to feel that ill again. It had been the worst virus or bug (or whatever it was) that I had experienced as an adult. I'm sure I had probably felt as bad with chickenpox as a kid, but I couldn't remember much about that.

The photocopier continued to jam, and, in the end, I lost my patience and simply gave up. Frank hadn't expressly forbidden me to take the originals home with me, after all, and, if the photocopier wasn't going to play ball, then I was going to put the originals in my rucksack and just not tell him what I had done. I couldn't see how they could come to any harm. I decided there was no reason to stay on campus, and that, perhaps, my best bet was to head for home. It was less than a week until Christmas, and there was no need for me to come back again before the holidays. The forecast was for snow later in the week, anyway, and I didn't really fancy walking on to campus unless I had to. I would send off an email to Frank when I got home, just so that he was kept informed of what I was doing. I was sure that he wouldn't object.

Just as I was about to leave, there was a knock on the door of the room. I put my rucksack back down and opened the door. In front of me was a young man, perhaps a few years younger than me.

"Can I help you?" I asked, probably sounding a little disgruntled at the interruption. All I wanted to do was go home.

"Hello," the man said. "I'm sorry to bother you, but are you the person working on the Taylor papers?"

"Yes, that's me."

"Ah, good. My name is Henry. I heard that you were working here. I wanted to come and say hello. I'm quite a big fan, you see? Of Alfred Taylor, that is."

Henry put out his hand, and I shook it.

"Jonathan. Jonathan Ballantyne," I said.

"I was wondering if we might be able to have a chat at some point about what you're doing? I'd be very interested in hearing about your work and what you've found out."

"I'm sure that could be arranged," I said. "Sometime at the beginning of next term, perhaps?"

I could see the disappointment on the young man's face.

"I was hoping to chat with you before then. Are you not coming back to campus this term?"

I shook my head.

"No. I was just leaving. I was ill a couple of weeks ago, and I'm still not feeling a hundred per cent, and so was going to give up and come back in the new year."

"Ah, I see," Henry said. His local accent was rather endearing. "Are you walking home? Perhaps I could walk with you, if you didn't mind?"

In all honesty, I *did* mind. Very much. But the young man in front of me seemed pleasant enough, and clearly very eager to hear about my work. And, if he was a fan of Taylor, then he might be of use to me in the future. He might even be a collector of Taylor items, if there was such a thing.

"We can walk if you'd like," I said. "I'm about a mile or so away. Just off Drager Avenue."

Henry smiled.

"I know where that is."

"Do you live close by?"

"Me? No. No, I live out in the sticks, I'm afraid. I wish I *did* live in the city."

"OK. Well, I'll just get my things, and then we'll be off."

I picked up my rucksack, and other bits and pieces, then we left the little room, and I locked the door. We walked down to the reception desk, and I handed the key to the woman who sat there.

"I won't be back until after Christmas," I told her, worried that I'd be chastised if I wasn't going to come in and not tell her in advance. "Have a good Christmas. And please tell Janice that I hope she gets well soon."

"I'm not going to see her," the woman said.

"Ah, well. Never mind, then."

We went out of the library, and started the walk home. I confess that I walked home faster than usual that day; the last thing I wanted at that precise moment was company. I was tired and just wanted to get home and, in all likelihood, go straight to bed. Somehow or other, I managed to be courteous to Henry, no matter how much I would have liked to have told him to leave me in peace.

"How far along with your project are you?" he asked me.

"Not very far, to be honest," I told him. "Most of what I've done so far has been sorting out all of the material."

"I see. I didn't realise there was that much."

"How did you find out that I was working on the project?"

Henry hesitated for a moment or two.

"I don't know," he said. "Just somewhere along the grapevine, as they say."

"Are you a student here?" I asked him.

"No, just an interested party."

He smiled at me, in an effort, I assume, to convince me that he was telling the truth. It didn't work. I could see from the outset that he was just telling a series of lies, and I didn't understand why. While few people at the university knew what I was doing, there was no real reason for it to have been kept a secret. Whoever had told him about it hadn't done anything wrong, even if I'd have preferred them to have sent me an email to let me know this chap was going to come to see me.

"How did you get interested in the works of Taylor?" I asked him.

"There are links to my family," he said. "My great grandfather knew him. He's dead now, but he told me about his friendship with him when I was a child. For some reason, it sparked something in me, and I started seeking out his works, after my parents inherited his records when he passed away."

The story sounded plausible enough, but still didn't seem *right*, but I wondered if I was just being paranoid in some way. Why on earth would this young man be lying to me? There was no reason. I knew that my depression when I was a student had made me somewhat paranoid, and I was beginning to get concerned that I could be heading into the same territory again.

"My grandfather even had the 78rpm release of the *Marlington Symphony*," Henry told me. "I had to buy a new turntable in order to play it."

"I think it's available on streaming services," I said. "Probably easier than playing it on 78s."

"I don't know about that. Did you know that it was the university orchestra playing on that first recording? Remarkable to think it was of a professional level back then, don't you think?"

I agreed that it was. The university orchestra during Taylor's tenure as head of music made a number of professional recordings, mostly of Taylor's own works with the composer conducting, but there were several other well-regarded recordings of works by other composers, too.

"Have you come across anything exciting during your research so far?" Henry asked me.

I wasn't sure how to answer that, especially as something about the *Festive Symphony* seemed…well…wrong. I didn't know how much I could trust him, but there didn't seem to be a real reason why I shouldn't. We were talking about the papers of a composer who had been dead for nearly eighty years, not top secret government documents.

"It's a bit early to say," I said. "I'm sure there will be some finds in the future. But I've only just started going through the scores. There's an interesting early piano sonata, but it's no masterpiece, that's for sure."

Henry looked disappointed.

"That's a shame," he said. "I was hoping there might be some lost masterpiece hidden away with all of those papers."

I looked across at him, and wondered if he knew something that he wasn't letting on. It was almost as if he already knew about the symphony and was trying to find out if I knew about it, too. But the notion was ridiculous. He might have been a fan of the composer's work, but how would he know about compositions that had never been played or written about? I was letting my imagination run away with me. That was clearly all it was.

Despite my suspicions about Henry, there was something about him that I had taken a liking to – which was something I wasn't expecting. He was good-looking, that was for sure, and charismatic, too. One of those people that walks into a room and everyone stops what they are doing – and yet, if anyone asked me to explain why I felt that way, I couldn't tell them.

We talked some more as we walked but, before

long, we found ourselves at my block of flats. Had I not been feeling so tired, I may have asked him inside. Henry had got my attention, even if I didn't really trust him, or believe what he had told me about his interest in Taylor. There was more to his story than what he had told me, but, by the time we had walked home, I didn't really care all that much about his lies, I just wanted to get to know him better.

"Well, this is me," I said, stopping outside my block of flats.

We stood there, not quite sure of what to say or do at that particular moment.

"You say that you're not coming back onto campus again before Christmas?" Henry asked.

I shook my head.

"No," I said. "I think I need a break from campus for a week or two."

Henry paused for a few seconds, before he asked:

"Would you like to meet tomorrow? For a drink, and to continue our conversation."

Despite my tiredness, I could feel my pulse quickening at the thought of seeing him once again. And yet, I wasn't sure if meeting him was the right thing to do. I might be interested in him, but was he interested in me? I wasn't sure. It had been so long since I had had my interest piqued about someone in that way that I wasn't certain of my talents in reading the situation correctly. I didn't want to make a complete idiot of myself.

"There's a pub," I found myself saying. "About

two hundred metres further down this road. The Black Horse. I could meet you there tomorrow evening, if you'd like. About eight o'clock?"

"Eight o'clock it is," Henry said, smiling.

"Right. Well…well, I'll see you tomorrow, then."

"Yes."

Not knowing what else to do or say, I simply said goodbye and went into the block of flats, not turning back to see if Henry was still standing there or if he had gone.

When I got in, I took the scores and diary out of my backpack, putting the scores on the music stand on the piano, and the diary on the coffee table in the living room, and then I sat down in my armchair and quickly fell asleep.

CHAPTER SEVEN

When I awoke, about two hours later, I felt somewhat refreshed, and less melancholy than I had during the day. Perhaps all I had needed, after all, was some sleep. I was hungry, too, and so I got out of the chair and walked through into the kitchen, and opened the fridge. There wasn't a great deal in there, and I made a note to myself that I should go out the next day and get some food. I wasn't all that bothered about buying extra for the Christmas period – shops were only shut for a couple of days, after all – but I did feel I should have something in the fridge in case the snow was as bad as the weather forecasts had suggested it might be. Most of the time, the weather didn't really deliver on such doom and gloom forecasts, but I didn't want to be caught out and end up living on toast for a week. I was due to visit my parents on the day after Boxing Day, and I was hoping that the weather would be good enough for me to go. I had already warned them that I might have to postpone until the new year if the snow got really bad.

There was a beef casserole ready meal in the fridge, and I pierced the film and put it in the microwave to heat up while I made myself a mug of tea. I ate the casserole while watching television, even though I couldn't find anything particularly interesting to watch, even if it was Christmas week. I'm not sure if it was a case of there not being anything on or whether I was just finding it difficult to settle down to anything. I ended up with a David Attenborough documentary, and, when it was over, I picked up the diary from the coffee table.

I skim-read the first entries, trying to find the first mention of the symphony. I got to the middle of January before I found what I was looking for.

January 18th,
It has been three months since the first performance of the piano concerto, and, I confess, I have not felt like composing in all of that time. I think the wretched, negative comments from the critics have affected me more than I would like to admit. I remember writing in my diaries that I would never take notice of what the critics say about my music, good or bad, but it appears it is not so easy as that, no matter how sincere my intentions were when I wrote that. I poured my heart and soul into the concerto, and seeing it mauled in that way was, I'm afraid to say, devastating. I even thought

at one point in the months since it was performed that I would never write again. Not a single musical idea was coming into my head during that time, and that was something which has not happened to me before.

Yesterday, however, I got a letter from Paris, asking if I would allow my concerto to be played there. The French have always been more enthusiastic about my music than the English, and I will, of course, give my permission for the work to be performed. I may even make the trip to hear it. The letter intimated that I could conduct it should I wish to.

I wonder if this news will give me a little more faith in my work once again. The confidence that I had in my abilities is most certainly not what it was, but, as my sister wrote to me only last week, the only way to get that confidence back is by starting on a new piece.

A local orchestra – although not a particularly good one, I might add – contacted me last year to ask if I might have something that they could use as the centrepiece of their Christmas concert this year. As I have no other offers, I think I might write a symphony for them.

What better way to come back from the embarrassing critiques of the concerto than with something larger and bolder? It will be a Festive Symphony, *with regular structure, but with themes from Christmas music rather than my own. I have ideas for that, and I believe I can probably compose it rather quickly. In fact, I think that is the only way. The longer I procrastinate over it, the more I am likely to doubt my own abilities. I will hunker down over the coming weeks, and cancel all of the forthcoming engagements that I can.*

The next few entries in the diary were of less interest, with Taylor making note of the engagements that he had cancelled, and moaning somewhat about the interruptions he was getting from friends and neighbours who had come to call without an invitation. I thought that I was unsociable, but Taylor beat me, hands down. The next entry of note came nearly a week later.

January 24th,
Rain. Lots of it. It's what I have been hoping for, as most people with any sense will remain indoors and not come to bother me. The last few days have been infuriating. I have wanted to work on the new piece, but never been left alone for more than five minutes at a time. I just wish people understood that writing music doesn't happen by itself. Finally, though, with the rain, and the peace it has brought me, I have been able to make some headway.

I have been sketching the first movement of the Festive Symphony *at the piano, and progress has been surprisingly swift. As usual, I will start from a piano arrangement and then orchestrate it at a later stage. I see no reason to change how I normally go about the process.*

I settled on the first and second theme of the first

movement as I saw Three Ships *and* Past Three o'Clock *respectively. They are, perhaps, better-known than what I was hoping for, but they fit together well, I think, and I have a good concept with regards to developing them. Perhaps I can find something a little more obscure for one of the later movements, although audiences might well prefer melodies that they already know. I suppose I have to decide if I am aiming for popular or critical success. Which is more important to me? I would like to say the former, but, unfortunately, it is the critics that have affected my morale and confidence. I am, at least, feeling a little buoyed by my efforts with the work so far, so perhaps this really is the piece with which I shall silence all of those who have doubted me.*

From what I had read of the diaries so far, Alfred Taylor seemed to be a lonely man, despite the fact that he was inundated with visitors (if his diaries were to be believed). He seemed to care nothing for the village life that he was a part of, and perhaps that was why he had thrived so much when he took up his position at the university about a decade later. He would have been surrounded by people who were genuinely interested in him for his music and opinions rather than for his fame.

    I could imagine him in 1914, though, getting more and more frustrated as the people of the village called on him, thinking him a man of leisure, just so that they could say they had had tea or drinks with the famous composer Alfred Taylor.

    In short, I felt sorry for him, despite his somewhat snobbish attitude.

CHAPTER EIGHT

Even as I write this account, I find it difficult to pinpoint when I first realised that something was wrong. I was, of course, well aware that my flu-like illness occurred within hours of finding the score of the symphony, and that I had also seen signs that the depression of my university days might be returning. This seemed more like bad luck to me than any consequence of the research that I was doing.

The illness had probably been caught on campus – the inevitable annual dose of what is generally referred to as "fresher's flu." As for the feeling of depression (if that *was* what I was feeling), I knew that I was prone to it, and working alone in a small room with no windows for a couple of months most certainly could have played a part in its recurrence.

However, there was something else going on, and I think I had been aware of it for several weeks, even if

I kept dismissing it. There had been the flickering lights in the room that I was working in when I came across the score of the *Festive Symphony*. And, then, the rattling of the door when I had first looked at the third movement. I had put both instances down to the gale-force winds at the time. And who is to say that it *wasn't* the wind? I couldn't prove that it *was*.

What bothered me a little more were the wet footprints going along the hall floor, and the day that the bath had filled up by itself. It was relatively easy to dismiss the flickering lights and rattling door, but not footprints coming from nowhere and a full bath of water.

But now, as I read the diary, I could hear water trickling from a tap. I got up from my chair and went to investigate. I tried the bathroom first, knowing that the taps in the sink were a little difficult to turn off fully, but there was nothing coming from them now. That left the kitchen, and, as I entered the room, I could see that the tap in there wasn't even dripping, let alone trickling. Even so, I went over to the sink to check, and gave the tap another half turn to make sure it was off. I couldn't hear the water running now, and so decided that, perhaps, it was coming from one of the pipes. I headed back for the living room, but, when I reached the kitchen door, I heard the tap behind me turn on, and water started to pour into the sink. I went back to the sink and turned the tap off again, rather bemused at how it could have happened. Perhaps there was something wrong with the tap. If it kept happening, I would tell the landlord, and hopefully he could get someone in to take a look at it.

I left the kitchen and went back into the living room, and picked up the diary again. As I did so, I heard quite distinctly the first three notes of the melody from the third movement of the symphony being played on the piano in my bedroom. They were played slowly – a couple of seconds each, but I knew what I was hearing. I got up quickly and went through into the bedroom, but, as I knew already, there was no-one there. How could there be? What's more, the piano was unplugged, and the plastic cover was over the keys. There was no way that the piano could have been played. Considering it was electric, it couldn't even be put down to changing temperatures affecting strings.

You might be thinking that I was simply hearing and seeing things, but I can assure you that was not the case. And I hadn't been drinking, either. I hadn't had a drink for months, and I was on no medication that could have caused me to hallucinate. Besides, there was still the issue of the bath and wet footprints from earlier.

I sat down on the bed, not sure of what to think. The incident had only added to my feeling that something strange was going on. I watched the piano, and waited for something else to occur.

"Play it again," I said, as if I was on a ghost-hunting programme on the television.

Nothing happened. I hadn't expected it to. I felt

like calling out again, asking if it was Alfred Taylor, but I felt like an idiot just for thinking of doing it. Besides, I was more than a little unnerved.

Alfred Taylor had not started haunting me because I was going through his papers.

The idea was absurd.

Or at least that was what I tried to tell myself.

The weather forecast had said that there might be snow showers, and so I went to the window and looked out. No snow. For that I was thankful. But, as I looked down at the street below, I saw a figure on the other side of the road, staring directly at my block of flats. It seemed that he was staring directly at me. I took a tissue from my pocket and wiped away the condensation so that I could see better, but, when I looked again, the figure had gone.

I chastised myself for being so stupid. He or she had probably just been waiting there for someone. I was giving myself the creeps, and so I went back into the living room to choose a record to play. I was tempted to pull out a piece by Taylor, but decided against it, and went for the Mozart *Horn Concertos* instead – something less brooding to try and lighten my mind. Sitting down, I flicked through the diaries, trying to find more details about the *Festive Symphony*, particularly the third movement. It meant flipping through several months of Taylor's rather bland updates on his work until I got to the end of April.

THE FESTIVE SYMPHONY

April 28th,

Someone in the village gave me several cuttings about music from The Telegraph *covering the last month or two. Not much of note, except that Elgar is being praised again, this time for his new choral songs. Are they really that much more impressive than my piano concerto that was criticised so harshly last year? I haven't heard them, of course, so I wouldn't know, but it seems to me that Elgar can do no wrong. He's even been making some recordings, I understand, with some more likely to come during the summer. I await an invitation to conduct some of my own compositions on a recording. I'm sure I will be waiting a long time. I feel rather badly for my comments about Elgar, for his popularity is not his fault. I have met him several times, and he has always been pleasant and complimentary to me about my work. I wonder if he says the same things in private. It is not his fault, either, that the critics in this country can't seem to cope with having more than one exceptional living British composer at a time.*

At least the Festive Symphony *is coming along nicely, even if I keep getting these blasted interruptions. The vicar (a rather dull individual that I cannot stand) called on me yesterday to ask if I would open the church fete again this year. I said that I would not, and that I was too busy. People have to realise that I have work to do, and cannot be at their beck and call to do a good deed here and to show my face there. Such appearances do not provide an income, and the people asking me to do these appearances would get quite a shock if I asked for a fee. More importantly, they simply distract me from composition.*

I have, therefore, decided that I will spend some time away during the summer months. I thought I would find somewhere to stay – a small inn, probably – in a place where people do not think they own a part of me. Norfolk, perhaps. We spent some holidays there when I was a child, and I should like to go back. As long as I can have a quiet room, and find a piano somewhere that I can use, I shall be happy to spend a few months getting the symphony finished. The second movement is now sketched out, but I still have no plans for the third. I need a main theme somewhat different to those in the other movements. Perhaps it will come to me while I am away, but I am well aware that I do not have much time to waste if the first performance is going to be just before Christmas.

CHAPTER NINE

The next morning, I awoke early to one of those crisp, cold days that almost makes the winter bearable. I'd much rather have the summer, I might add. Night closing in at four o'clock in the afternoon is not something I like, but sunny-yet-cold days at least give me the impetus to *do* something.

I had some cereal and a couple of cups of coffee, and then got a bus to the nearest Sainsbury, so that I could stock up on what I would need if the snow that had been forecast actually arrived. I had my doubts. Marlington rarely plays ball with the weather forecasters.

Supermarkets are never my favourite place to go to, and that visit was particularly awful. Half of Marlington seemed to be there, no doubt stocking up for both the Christmas period and the possibility of bad weather. The schools had already broken up for the

Christmas break and so there were kids running around the shop as well, which made things even worse. I got what I wanted as quickly as I could, but bought more than I was planning to, and realised that I wouldn't be able to carry it home if I went by bus, and so ordered a taxi, which took nearly forty minutes to arrive. I promise you, Marlington is a lovely place, but the public transport and taxi services are bloody awful.

I got home around lunchtime, and, after putting the shopping away, heated up some soup, so I could eat the fresh crusty rolls that I had just bought, as, within half a day, they would become so hard that they could be used as paperweights or cricket balls.

I watched the news while I ate my lunch, and then decided that I would spend some of the afternoon reading through some more of the diaries. I had got to the point where Alfred Taylor had decided to go and stay in Norfolk, and had realised that this would probably have been the first time that he saw the city of Marlington that would later become his home. It was unlikely that he would spend time in Norfolk in 1914 and not visit such a historic city.

Before I picked up the diary, I went back over to the window. If anyone had asked me why, I would have said that it was to keep an eye on what the weather was doing, but that would have been a lie. The real answer was that I was checking to see if the figure from the night before had returned. I wasn't really sure why he or she had disturbed me so much, or made me so jittery, but I just felt that my nerves were on edge after the serious of strange things had been occurring. I tried to tell myself that the person standing outside the night before was probably just someone looking up at another window, or waiting for a friend, but the problem was that my mind was somehow connecting him to the figure in the dream that I'd had on the day I had become ill. That lone figure in the audience. I even thought it was creepy that I could remember the dream so well several weeks later.

I forced myself to move away from the window. I couldn't spend half the day looking for someone (something?) that was never likely to come back. And, even if he did return, what business was it of mine?

I went back to my armchair, and opened the diary.

May 16th,
I am in Norfolk.

The journey was long and dull, and the train somewhat full. I managed to read some of the newspaper, but my concentration kept getting interrupted by the noise of those around me. I had been hoping to get a carriage to myself, but that was clearly too much to ask for. At least I'll have plenty of solitude in the coming weeks.

I finally arrived at the village at around 5pm. There was rather a long wait at Marlington station before my connection. The owner of the inn had arranged for me to be met at the nearest station, which was a good mile or so from Standham, the village in which I am staying.

Standham, I realise now, is very small indeed, and, at most, half the size of my own village. As we travelled through it, towards the inn in which I am staying, I wondered if I had made a mistake, and that it might just be too quiet for me, but I chastised myself for thinking that way. The more peaceful the surroundings, the better. I wanted to be left alone to work, after all.

The room at the inn is basic, but comfortable enough, and the supper provided was hot and hearty, if a little rustic. I believe I will be dining on stews and suchlike a great deal in the coming weeks. I fear I shall put on a substantial amount of weight by the time I go home.

I asked at the inn about where I might find a piano that I could use in the village. They looked at me at first as if they had never heard of the instrument, but then I realised that it was merely a strange request for a guest at the inn. Clearly my name was not familiar to the owners, and I do not know whether I am happy about that or mildly disappointed that my fame has not reached deepest, darkest Norfolk. At least it means that I will not be interrupted in my work in the way that I am at home. The woman behind the bar at the inn suggested that I go to see the local teacher, to see if I might use the piano at the school during the evenings and at the weekends.

After supper, I walked through the village (this did

not take long) and stopped by at the house of the teacher, a rather kindly woman from what I have seen so far, by the name of Agatha Adams. She asked me in and offered me a hot cup of tea and some cake, which was most welcome as the evening had turned somewhat chilly. She also introduced me to her son, a handsome youth of about twenty-one or twenty-two, I should say. Edgar. Edgar works at a local farm, apparently. I was told that the surrounding farms employ most of the men in the village.

I'm pleased to say that Agatha was aware of my name and reputation as a composer, and seemed rather excited by my presence. She was only too keen to allow me to use the school piano when it wasn't in use. However, she said it was badly in need of tuning, and might not be of much use to me. But she also had a piano at her home, she said, and that I was welcome to use it as and when I wanted, and that she would leave a key out for me if I thought I might want to play it when she and Edgar were out. I told her that she was very kind, and that, yes, that would be a welcome arrangement, not least because she and her son would not have to listen to me if they were not at home. I offered to pay Agatha for the use of her piano, but she refused, saying that she would be honoured to have a famous composer playing it. I believe that we will become fast friends during my stay in the village, and I thought I might dedicate the new symphony to her in gratitude.

I put the diary down, and went through into the bedroom to take a look at the score of the *Festive Symphony*, which was on the piano music stand. As I remembered, there was no dedication at all on the front page. I wondered what had changed Taylor's mind about dedicating it to Agatha Adams. Perhaps later diary entries would give me an answer.

Reading the rest of them would have to wait. Clara was coming to visit me the next day, and I knew that she would berate me if it was Christmas Eve and I didn't have any Christmas decorations up. I didn't have many, and I always assumed that I was not alone in that. Do men living on their own normally bother with such things if they're not going to get visited by kids? Either way, I knew it was much easier to hang up the decorations I had rather than listening to Clara moaning at me about not doing it. I even tried to get in the Christmas spirit by putting Saint-Saens' *Oratorio de Noel* in the CD player while I worked. I had sung it in a concert one Christmas, where it had been paired with Britten's *Saint Nicholas*. It had been the last time that I had sung in a choir, and hearing it again made me nostalgic for the experience. Perhaps I would re-join the university choir once Christmas was over. That would please Clara, too.

There was another reason for playing music that afternoon. The flat seemed horribly quiet. Despite being on a busy road, there was very little traffic that day, and I didn't even hear my upstairs neighbours moving around, or the soft murmur of their television.

THE FESTIVE SYMPHONY

I couldn't remember my flat ever being that quiet, and it made me a little nervous. I doubt it would have done had it not been for recent events – most notably the piano playing by itself. At least I wouldn't hear it if I had music playing. Or that was my hope, at least.

CHAPTER TEN

By the time I finished putting up the decorations, it was late afternoon, and I decided to have my dinner a little early as I was meeting Henry that night, something which I was looking forward to with eagerness. To my surprise, he had been almost constantly on my mind since the day before, and I kept telling myself that I was acting like an idiotic teenager experiencing their first crush. It clearly *was* a crush, even though I tried to convince myself that I was just looking forward to talking over my work with someone else who had the same enthusiasm for it as I did. However, this kind of interest in another person was something that I was not used to, and my stomach grumbled with nervousness, and I felt my hands begin to tremble slightly each time I thought of him.

The idea was utterly stupid, of course. I'd had no indication that Henry was interested in me, or even that he was gay. For all I knew, he had a wife and kids back in…where did he say he lived? I realised he hadn't told me. In fact, he hadn't told me anything about himself, and had actively avoided my question about where he had found out about my work.

I reminded myself that we had talked for less than half an hour – hardly enough time for him to tell me his life story.

Despite that, I still arrived at the White Horse twenty minutes early that night, and I was pleased when Henry walked in only ten minutes later.

"You're early!" he said, smiling, as he sat down at my table.

"So are you," I told him.

"You were here before me, though."

I bought us our drinks, and then sat down again.

"Cheers," Henry said.

"Cheers," I replied.

We clinked our glasses and drank.

"What have you been doing today?" Henry asked.

"Some work – reading through Taylor's diaries. And then getting some decorations up for Christmas."

"Are the diaries interesting?"

I wasn't quite sure how to answer, given that I hadn't told him about the discovery of the symphony.

"Reasonably. I'm on 1914 at the moment."

"Ah," Henry said, "that was the year when he first came to this part of the country, wasn't it?"

"How did you know about that?"

"I don't know," Henry said. "I must have read it

somewhere. One of the biographies, I reckon."

"Not your great grandfather?" I asked.

"I don't know. Possibly."

"Did he know Taylor well? How were they friends?"

Henry hesitated for a moment or two before answering.

"He knew him at the university."

I had been thinking about Henry's tale about his great grandfather knowing Alfred Taylor, and was trying to work out how that was possible. Taylor had died in 1942, and Henry was surely no older than his early twenties, meaning he would have been born around 2000. Taylor stepped back from most of his university duties around 1940 due to ill health, and so that meant Henry's great grandfather need to have been eighteen or so by 1939 at the very latest, and that would have made him around ninety by the time Henry was ten. It was possible, of course, but somehow it seemed unlikely to me that, at aged ten, Henry was so taken by the stories of his great grandfather's friendship with an out of fashion composer that he started to buy the records of Taylor. Something just didn't seem right, but I was unable to work out what it was, or why Henry might be lying to me about such a thing.

And yet, as we chatted that evening, I didn't really care much that I was being lied to. I was just happy to be in Henry's company, and he seemed to be happy to be in mine.

THE FESTIVE SYMPHONY

"Are the diaries very revealing?" he asked me.

"Not yet," I said. "But I don't know what I would expect them to reveal. He comes across as rather unsociable, in all honesty. Much preferring his own company than that of other people. Although I can sympathise with him in that regard."

Henry looked across at me, as if hurt by what I had said.

"Present company excepted," I added, quickly.

"Of course," Henry said, with a smile. "I'm guessing the diaries explain why he came this way at that time?"

"Yes. He wanted some peace and quiet, if we believe what he has written. He had a new piece that he was trying to work on, and he got fed up with interruptions from the villagers where he lived, and endless invites to open fêtes, and so on. That was why he stayed in Standham for a few months. But I'm only at just after Easter in the diary. He's only just arrived there."

"He chose well," Henry said. "Standham is a nice place."

"You know it well?" I asked.

"I live there," he said.

This took me aback somewhat. I wasn't expecting that.

"Alfred Taylor's visit is still probably the most important thing that happened there," Henry went on. "It's just a tiny village. Not much bigger than it was a hundred years ago, although there's going to be a housing Estate built about a mile away."

"He stayed in the inn in the village. Is it still there?" I asked.

"Yes, of course. Not much changes in those kinds of Norfolk villages, I promise you."

"I would like to visit Standham at some point. Would you show me around?"

"Of course, but there's not much to see."

"Thank you. We can sort something out in the new year."

The evening passed quickly. The conversation was easy and relaxed, most of it about Alfred Taylor, but not all of it. I told him a little bit about my life, and how I ended up researching a thesis on the composer. Henry also told me a bit about his own life, but was still rather vague about his background, and I ended the evening not knowing much more about him than I did at the start. Strangely, I was neither surprised or disappointed by this. Henry was the mysterious type, and I found that rather attractive for some reason. I found *most* things about Henry attractive.

Two-and-a-half hours later, we walked out of the pub, and stood there on the street rather awkwardly, not sure of how to proceed from there. My body was telling me quite clearly how *I* wanted to proceed at that moment, but I didn't have the self-confidence to act upon it. I could imagine Clara telling me off for being a fool and not taking advantage of the situation, and, at that point, I decided I would not tell her about Henry unless I absolutely had to.

THE FESTIVE SYMPHONY

After a few seconds of silence, I made my move.

"Can I have your phone number?" I asked him.

It was a rather bold question for me, but at least I could make out that I wanted to stay in touch because of the Taylor connection if it turned out that he wasn't interested in me for any other reason.

"I...I don't have it with me," he said. "And I don't remember the number."

To say I was disappointed is something of an understatement. This seemed like nothing more than an excuse, and I was sure that, if he turned out his pockets, there would be a mobile phone in them. Well, at least I had tried, and not made a fool of myself by asking him up to my flat, only for him to say no. That would have been embarrassing.

"I'm sorry," he said. "But we can meet again, if you'd like. How about next week? Here. On Tuesday. Would that be OK?"

I was relieved. Perhaps he *had* simply left his phone at home, after all. It seemed an odd thing for him to do, but I was willing to give him the benefit of the doubt.

"Yes. That's good for me," I said. "I was going to my parents, but I have put if off because of the bad weather they have forecast. Eight o'clock again?"

"Perfect."

I wanted to move in to kiss him as we said our goodbyes, but didn't have the courage, and we made do with a handshake instead. I wished him a merry Christmas, and then turned and walked back towards my flat. After a few seconds, I turned around to get one last look at him, but he was already gone.

CHAPTER ELEVEN

May 18th,

When I arrived here a couple of days ago, I was not expecting to be treated so quickly to such wonderful weather, with it being so early in the season.

Yesterday was my day for unpacking and getting used to my new surroundings that are going to be my home for what could be several months. Today, however, I settled down to work. I had my breakfast at the inn, and then went back to my room and sat at my desk with the score for the second movement, and went through it to make sure I was happy with it, and making several corrections and changes. I really am convinced that it is the finest thing I have yet written, and I believe that this symphony will unite both critics and the public in praise. Even the appallingly difficult music critic in The Telegraph *will soon be singing my praises, I am sure of it.*

THE FESTIVE SYMPHONY

The third movement is causing me more difficulty, however. I still do not have my main theme for it, and, without that, it is impossible to make headway, and so I started sketching out the fourth movement instead. I can always return to the third at a later date. Inspiration will strike, I am sure of it. I worked for a couple of hours in my room after lunch, and then decided to take advantage of the Adams's piano. The walk through the village was most pleasant, and the hot weather allowed for me to go out in just my shirt sleeves.

The village is much quieter and smaller than the one back home and, while Mrs. Adams is a teacher at the village school, I cannot imagine that she has many children to teach. A couple of dozen at most. The men of the village were in the fields that I passed on the way to Mrs. Adams's house, and, making the most of the hot weather, they were stripped to the waist in most cases, with the sun beating down upon their backs.

I let myself in to the Adams house, and played through the opening bars of the fourth movement, and then worked on filling in the orchestral parts. I had been there about an hour or two when the door opened and young Edgar walked in.

"Good day, Mr. Taylor," he said, when he saw me seated at the piano. "It is a lovely day, don't you think?"

I looked up from my work, and smiled at him.

"Indeed. Most unusual for this time in the year," I said.

"It was like this here for much of April, too," he said.

I could see that for myself, as his bare torso was tanned in a way that couldn't have resulted from simply one day working in the sun.

"It must be hot in the fields," I said.

"Oh, we manage," he told me. "Much better than working in the rain." He paused for a moment. "Well, I should go and clean up," he said. "Mother gets riled if I'm not clean and tidy for supper. Will you be joining us, Mr. Taylor?"

"Thank you, but no," I said. "I am thankful enough for the use of your piano, and so will refuse the offer to eat your food as well."

Edgar nodded at me, and went back outside. I was tempted to make an excuse to follow him, so that we could continue our conversation while I watched him wash. However, my nerves got the better of me, and so I stayed where I was and packed up my things so that I was ready to leave when he came back in. As I walked back to the inn that evening, I chastised myself for getting in a fluster over the young man. I'm not sure what came over me. I believe I see so little of youth at home that it holds some kind of attraction for me when I come across it in that way. I am sure that young Edgar will make a fine husband for a young woman someday.

May 19th,
The lovely weather continues, and a farmer told me in

the inn last night that it looks set to continue for quite a while. I'm not sure how he can be so definite about that, but country types appear to get some kind of intuition about such things, I suppose.

My plan was to stay at the inn today and continue working here, but, by the afternoon, I was eager to go out into the sun, and so walked through the village once again to Agatha and Edgar's home. I have rather taken a liking to their small cottage, which can barely be big enough for the two of them, and yet it is so welcoming – much more so than my own abode back home. I am beginning to believe that my own house if too large for me. I wonder if I might be more comfortable in a small cottage.

Agatha arrived home first this evening.

"I could hear the piano as I walked along the road," she said. "I'm glad you're finding it useful."

"I would find it very hard to do my work without it," I told her. "I must reiterate that I am more than willing to pay you for the use of it. I realise that it must be an inconvenience having me here."

"Not at all," Agatha said, and offered me some tea and a piece of cake, which I accepted with thanks. "I think you must have made quite an impression on Edgar," she went on. "He said this morning that he might want me to teach him to play the piano. I tried for years when he was younger to get him interested in it, and he wouldn't have any of it. Now, suddenly, he wants to play. Better late than never, so they say, but I have so little time, these days."

THE FESTIVE SYMPHONY

"I would be more than happy to teach him, if you would like," I said. "I have taught piano in the past, and it would repay you for the use of your instrument."

"That's very kind of you, Mr. Taylor, but I'm not so sure he's really committed to it. I think it's only just because you're here, and your work has got him interested."

Edgar came in a few minutes later, and kissed his mother on her cheek.

"Edgar! You're full of sweat," she said.

"I'll wash up in a minute," he said. "Good day, Mr. Taylor. Have you made much progress today?"

"Some," I said, tapping the manuscript in front of me.

"What is it that you are working on?" Agatha asked me.

I told her about the Festive Symphony, and a little bit about how it was structured, and what melodies I was using for the main themes. I managed to hold their attention as I did so, and their enthusiasm for what I was trying to achieve was most welcome.

"Are you just here for work?" Agatha asked, afterwards.

"Mostly," I said. "But I thought I would like to do some walking while the weather continues as it is."

"Well, there are plenty of places to walk around here. Some of the paths go on for miles. I'm sure Edgar could take you on some interesting walks, if you'd like?"

The thought of going on a walk with Edgar

pleased me immensely, and he genuinely seemed happy to come with me, and so we have arranged such an expedition for the day after tomorrow, which I am very much looking forward to.

CHAPTER TWELVE

"So was the attraction between Taylor and Edgar a mutual thing?" Clara asked.

It was mid-afternoon on Christmas Eve. Clara had arrived an hour or so earlier, and had been eager for me to tell her how the research was going. Despite us both being at the same university, we had barely seen each other since I had moved back to Marlington. This was mostly my fault. I was the one who failed to respond to her texts and messages about grabbing a coffee together, and so this was the first chance that I'd had to tell her how things were going.

"I'm not sure," I said. "It's difficult to tell through his diaries. And we only have Taylor's opinion anyway, and he's a bit of a grouch who tended to feel a bit sorry for himself, and is an horrendous snob. But it's not like they were the same age. Taylor would have been in his forties by that point, and the lad was only twenty or so. The last entry that I've read through *does* tell us that Edgar taught Taylor the melody that was used in the third movement of the symphony."

"The movement that's scribbled over?"

"Yeah. They went on their walk, and Edgar took them down to the river. He asked Taylor about his work, and apparently Edgar sang this melody to him, telling him it was a lullaby traditionally sung by the people of the village to their kids as they went to sleep on Christmas Eve. It would have been exactly what Taylor was looking for."

"That's interesting. So, what is the tune?"

"The music's on the piano in the bedroom, if you want to take a look. I'll show you later, but the melody isn't particularly exciting, although it is a little strange. More modal than tonal. But we do only have those few bars that escaped Taylor's apparent rage."

I paused for a moment, wondering how much more I should say. Clara sensed that I was holding something back. She could read me like a book.

"I feel there's a 'but' coming on," she said.

"It's just that…"

I hesitated for a moment, not sure that I wanted to tell Clara about the things that had been happening.

"*Tell me,*" she said.

"There's something weird about it," I said. "About the entire thing. The scribbled over manuscript, and the tune itself. Plus, strange things have started happening since I came across it."

"What kind of strange things?"

THE FESTIVE SYMPHONY

I took a deep breath, not really sure what Clara would say in response to what I was about to tell her.

"The bath filling up by itself. Wet footprints coming out of nowhere in the hallway. Odd dreams. The piano playing on its own."

"You're kidding?"

I shook my head.

"No, not at all."

"Are you saying you're being haunted, Jonathan?"

"I'm not sure I'd go that far. It feels like such a stupid thing to say. But there's something weird about that melody, and this man that Taylor very quickly took a liking to when he arrived in Norfolk. I'm hoping the diaries will give more of the secrets away, but I'm not making as much progress with them as I'd like. Every time I start reading the damned things, I fall asleep. And the dreams are just…weird. I think it's fear of the dreams that is stopping me just sitting down and reading the rest of the diary in one go."

"Are they nightmares?"

"I suppose so. They are just very, very unsettling. Everything about it is unsettling, and it has kind of crept up on me. I didn't take much notice of it at first, partly because I found the manuscript on the day I got the flu, or whatever it was. So I put some of it down to that. Having a temperature can cause you to dream or imagine all sorts of things. But it's still going on."

Clara sat quietly for a few seconds.

"Say something," I said to her. "Tell me I'm not losing it."

"It's not that," she said. "I just feel bad that it was me who persuaded you to come back this way and take on the project."

"Don't feel bad about that. I'm enjoying the work, to be honest. It's just these added extras that I'm not so keen on. It's all linked to this bloody piece of music. Part of me wishes I'd never found it."

"What are the dreams about?" Clara asked.

"The first one had me playing violin in the university orchestra, and I was playing the melody of that movement of the symphony. And everybody walked out of the concert while I kept playing. The only person left in the audience was this mysterious figure, and it started coming towards me."

"Jesus. That's horrible," Clara said.

"I dreamed that on the night I fell ill, so I just assumed it was caused by a fever. But it wasn't. I've had similar ones since."

"What makes you think that Taylor and this Edgar chap are connected to them?"

I shrugged my shoulders.

"I'm not sure. But the *sense* of them is there. It's hard to explain. But let's change the subject. It's Christmas Eve. I don't want to be thinking about that today."

When I went into the kitchen to make us another drink, I saw that it was snowing quite heavily.

"The snow's arrived," I said, when I took our coffees through into the living room. "It's coming down quite heavily."

"OK. I'd better drink this and go, I suppose. I don't like driving in the snow much."

"It's funny how everyone wants a white Christmas," I said, "and then, when we actually have one, we start moaning about it because we're not able to go out and see the people we want to."

"Yeah," Clara said. "I hope I'm able to get to Mum's tomorrow. I don't want her spending Christmas on her own – not after the last two were buggered up by Covid. What are you doing tomorrow?"

"Nothing. I'll be here on my own. I'm fine by that."

"Unsociable bastard," Clara said, smiling.

"That's me! I was meant to go to visit Mum and Dad, but I've postponed it because of the weather."

"Just make sure you don't sit here working. Or reading that bloody diary. The thought of it is giving me the creeps from what you've told me."

"There isn't much more to read, to be honest. It cuts off halfway through the year, and he didn't write any more in a diary until two or three years later – unless there is some missing, but I doubt that, to be honest. He definitely gave it up in mid-1914 for some reason."

"Perhaps it would have got too steamy for him to write as he got friendlier with this young man."

"I really hope he doesn't write about that kind of thing. The thought of Alfred Taylor in bed sounds just as frightening as the figure I keep dreaming about."

Clara left for home about half an hour later. I walked her out to her car, and the snow was falling heavily by that point. I was a little worried about her driving home – not that Clara was a bad driver, but there were plenty of idiots on the road, especially on Christmas Eve.

"Text me when you get home," I said.

"You're a worryguts," she replied, with a smile.

I didn't deny this.

I watched her drive off, and then walked back towards the flat. As I did so, one of my neighbours came out to put some things in the bin.

"Merry Christmas," I said, as I held the door open for her.

"Thank you, you too. Are you settling in OK?"

"Yeah. Everything's fine," I said. I paused for a moment before saying: "There's just one thing. Have you had any problem with the water in the building?"

She shook her head.

"I can't say that I have. What kind of problems?" she asked.

"Just the taps seem to be turning on by themselves."

"Oh, that'll be the washers. You should speak to the landlord and get them in about it. You don't want to be using water you don't need now we're all on water meters."

I said that, yes, it must be the washers, and then went back upstairs to my flat.

CHAPTER THIRTEEN

Despite what I might have implied to Clara, my plan for the rest of Christmas Eve was to get to the end of the diary. There were still a number of entries left to read, but I had decided that I would skim-read them for the most part, and just concentrate on the ones which seemed important.

First, however, I wanted to relax for a bit. I had expected my depression to get worse as the week went on, but it hadn't happened yet. It was still there, lurking in the background, but it wasn't causing me major problems just yet, with the exception of feeling tired. Having company all afternoon, even when it was a friend like Clara, wore me out. I didn't have to put on a show around her – didn't have to pretend I was feeling better than I was. After all, she'd seen me at my very worst in the past, but, even so, the act of chatting for two or three hours was exhausting for me in itself.

I had a choice of having a long, relaxing soak in the bath, or going to bed for a couple of hours. I decided that the bath would ultimately be quicker, and leave me more time to finish off the diary. I went through into the bathroom, turned on the taps, and poured a rather generous amount of bubble bath under the running water.

The water pressure in the flat was not the greatest, and so I knew it would take about ten minutes to fill the bath up. I walked through into the kitchen and made myself a hot chocolate to take with me into the bath, and then went to find a CD to play as I soaked. I felt that I should be playing Christmas music, but that wasn't what I was in the mood for, and so put a disc of Scriabin's *Piano Concerto* in the disc tray. It had been one of the set works for study at A-Level, and I fell in love with it back then, and had remained very fond of it as the years had passed. When something is troubling us, we so often return to a film we know inside out, or re-read a favourite book. I always returned to certain pieces of music, and this was one of them.

Back in the bathroom, the water had now filled most of the tub, and I turned the taps off, and undressed. I took my clothes through to the bedroom, set the CD playing, and then got into the bath. I lay back and rested my head on the back of the tub, while the music floated down the hallway. I breathed in deep, and closed my eyes, knowing that the bath would make me feel relaxed and less stressed.

I tried to just clear my mind, and not think of anything, but I had to actively fight against thoughts of Alfred Taylor filling my head. My mind didn't seem to be keen on forgetting, just for a short while, what I had been reading in the diaries. It was, perhaps, inevitable. Even so, each time those thoughts invaded my mind, I pushed them away. I wanted to forget Taylor, just for an hour. And, more than anything, I wanted to forget the odd things that had been happening since I had come across the symphony.

After a few minutes, I opened my eyes and reached down beside the bath to get my mug of chocolate. I took a drink, replaced the mug on the floor, and lay back again. As I did so, I heard a notification sound on my phone which I had left in the bedroom. I assumed it was just Clara, telling me she had got home safely. The slow movement of the concerto was now playing, and I concentrated on the lush romantic sounds coming from the CD player.

At some point shortly after, I must have dozed off. I awoke after only a few minutes to hear the concerto coming to an end. I waited for the next piece to begin, having forgotten what music took up the second half of the disc. After a few seconds, the music began again, and it made me sit up in the bath. The music I was hearing was the first movement of the *Festive Symphony* – a piece of music that had never been performed or recorded, and which, in all likelihood, nobody other than myself had seen in eighty years. I waited for a moment or two, expecting the music I was hearing to be just the remnants of a dream. But it continued. I knew my chances of relaxing in the bath were over, and so I stood up quickly and got out of the bath, not caring that more water than usual made its way on to the bathroom floor as I did so. Wet and naked, I walked through into the bedroom. By the time I got there, the music had changed to a symphony by Scriabin, not the *Festive Symphony* by Taylor. I turned the disc off. I didn't want to hear any more.

Had I imagined it? I knew I had not. I felt that the playing of Taylor's music through the CD was a challenge to me: finish the diary, or else.

Or else what?

Or else I'm coming for you.

What on earth would put that idea in my head? *Who* was going to come for me? Taylor? No, that didn't seem right. I felt that I was being haunted, but it wasn't by Alfred Taylor. But, if not him, *who*?

I went back into the bathroom to get dry and to empty the bath of water. There was a dead body in the bath. The naked body of a man. I saw it, just for an instant before it disappeared, and the bath returned to how I had left it. I pulled out the plug, and left the room as quickly as I could, wondering how much longer I could stay in the flat if such things continued. But would leaving the flat help? I wasn't the flat that was being haunted, it was *me*.

CHAPTER FOURTEEN

May 25th,

I have been neglecting my diary somewhat over the last few days, partly because I have been making so much progress with the symphony, and partly because I have been enjoying my current surroundings. I have only been here a week, but it feels much longer, and I truly feel at home. The locals are kind to me, and have struck up conversations with me in the inn during the evenings, and Agatha and Edgar have been most welcoming. Most importantly, nobody wants anything from me.

I have tried to get myself into a routine of working on the symphony during the day, and then going for a walk with young Edgar during the early evening, but sticking to that routine is something that I am finding difficult. There are distractions. He seems to be most interested in my work, and clearly honoured that I have used the melody he sang to me on our first walk as the main theme for the third movement. He is a most remarkable young man, and our friendship is making my time here in Norfolk particularly enjoyable.

The warm weather continues, and the river where Edgar invariably takes me walking seems to be used regularly by the youth of the village for swimming during the hot weather. Edgar is a fine swimmer, and seemed somewhat surprised when I told him that I did not know how to swim. He has offered to show me, but I have never liked bodies of water very much, and so am unlikely to take him up on his generous offer, especially as some of the other young men from the village are by the river when we go for our walks. I don't wish to humiliate myself in front of them. I would much rather watch them enjoy themselves.

I feel there is some kind of tension between them and Edgar, as if he is not liked or, perhaps, that they make fun of him. Edgar says I am imagining things, but I am not so sure of that. Men of that age can be very cruel when they want to be, and Edgar is of a sensitive nature. He is just the type of person that these young men might ridicule, and sometimes he may even be the subject of the joke and doesn't realise it. I know this from my own experiences when I was at school. I had no idea that others were laughing behind my back until someone told me. In some ways, I wish they had kept quiet, and thus left me blissfully ignorant, for my time at school from that point was miserable and, I feel, left me with a lack of confidence, even about the things I know that I am good at. I have no doubt that this is why the harsh critics affect me so.

May 29th,
I realise that I have written less and less in my diary of late. I note that it is now four days since my last entry. I feel that this might be because my days here are becoming less governed by routine than they are when I am at home. Here in Norfolk, I have fallen into the habit of getting up when I wish rather than when I think I should – something that seems to confuse the innkeepers, I might add. Likewise, I no longer have a regular time for when I go to bed. Sometimes it is nine or ten o' clock, and, others, it is in the early hours of the morning.

There are so many things praying on my mind that I sometimes find it hard to relax enough for sleep. I seem to find it easier to work in the late evenings here, whereas I would work during the afternoon back home. My mind seems to provide me with all kinds of wonderful ideas about my work at the least likely times just now. Last evening, I was already in bed when inspiration struck, and I could not stop myself from getting out of bed in my night clothes and sitting at my desk, writing some of the best, most sweetest, music of my life. I am absolutely positive that this will be my masterwork, and I am rather frustrated that I cannot put into words for you, my diary, why I think that, other than that being around Edgar has something to do with it. I went twenty-fours without seeing him a couple of days ago, and I wrote nothing. Absolutely nothing. I have no explanation for it, other than that Edgar has become a kind of muse. His boyish enthusiasm rubs off on me, and, I confess, I feel rather honoured to be in his company.

Edgar seems utterly relaxed around me. We walk for several miles most evenings, and then sit and rest and talk for an hour or so before making our way back to the village. It was rather late when we returned a few nights back, and Agatha scolded us both as if we were naughty children, telling us that she was worried that something might have happened to us, although I have no idea what she thinks could possibly happen here in Standham.

June 3rd,
I have resolved to write in the diary just when I have enough news of interest to do so. When I am working hard on the symphony, and it is coming along well, I do not want to break my concentration to spend half an hour or so recording the more banal elements of my life.

However, tonight I went walking with Edgar, as we usually do. I sat down by the river and watched him undress and wade in, marvelling at just how strongly he can swim. When he emerged from the river, he climbed up the bank and sat on the grass, waiting for the evening sun to dry him before he got dressed. I cannot think what came over me, but I leaned in towards him and kissed him gently on his lips.

I apologised as soon as I had done it, knowing that it was something I should not have done – and I was not even entirely sure why I had. I cannot fathom why I would act in that way with another man – even one whose company I appreciate as much as Edgar's. The strange thing is that Edgar did not react badly. He did not return the kiss, but simply put his hand over mine, and smiled. He then stood up and got dressed, and said that we should be making our way back home if we wanted to avoid another telling off by his mother.

We walked home in silence, neither of us knowing what to say to the other. Then, since I got back here, I have sat on my bed going over what happened, trying to work out why I had behaved in that way, Is it that I feel something towards this young man? Is that even possible? I have heard of such cases, of course. I'm sure all men of the world have, but to think that I… No, it simply is not possible. I have never felt that way about another man, and, surely, by my age I would have done so by now? True, of course, I have never married, but I have had experiences with women – some of them have even been very pleasant.

I really would like to get some sleep – I'm sure that would help me make sense of it – but my mind is not willing as yet to stop whirling, and so I am sitting here, writing everything down, in the hope that it will make me understand what has happened. Yet, all I can think of is the boy swimming in the river, turning to smile at me on the bank as he goes past. It is such a pleasant image.

I think I might go and find the innkeeper and see if I can trouble him for a drink of whiskey or brandy to try to help me sleep. I can still hear him and his wife moving about, and so they are obviously not asleep as yet. I am hoping that everything will make more sense to me in the morning, and also that I have not lost Edgar's friendship, for I am not sure if I can stay here if that is the case.

June 7th,
I have not seen Edgar since the incident a few days ago. I feel unable to forgive myself for what I did, and I have not been able to face him, even to apologise.

Agatha visited me at the inn today, asking me why I have not been to see her son after previously seeing him almost every day. She said that he was disappointed and hurt by my avoiding him. I could not tell her the truth for my absence, of course. That is not something I can discuss with a woman, even one I have grown to respect as much as Agatha Adams.

But there was another reason for her visit. She told me that she had overheard gossip in the village about my friendship with Edgar. "I cannot repeat what I heard said," she told me, but I can imagine to what she is referring. The local lads had been down at the river on a couple of occasions when we were there, and I fear that they might have misconstrued what they saw. It doesn't take long for gossip to spread through a village, whether it is true or false. By the time everyone has heard it, the truth is no longer important, for it is the rumours that will be believed.

"I think we should stop our association with you entirely, Mr. Taylor," she said. "Especially since you appear to have stopped it temporarily of your own volition. I don't wish for you to tell me whether the gossip is true or false. That is not my concern. I do not believe that you have intentionally harmed my son, and I realise it is perfectly possible that he gave you…encouragement…in whatever might have happened. However, you must not see him again."

I nodded my head, and said that I understood. I didn't try to deny whatever the gossip was in the village. I was not going to lie to the woman. She deserves more respect than that. I promised her that I would not see either of them again, and, after she had left, I informed the innkeepers that I would be leaving for home tomorrow.

I turned through the pages in the diary, but, for the next couple of weeks, there were no entries at all. Taylor had next written an entry at the end of June. It was just a few lines in length.

June 29th,
I received the news today that young Edgar is dead. The news came in the form of a short, but polite, letter from his mother. She states that he accidentally drowned in the river last week, and has asked me not to attend the funeral. But how could Edgar drown? He was an expert swimmer; I saw plenty of evidence of

that.

I turned the pages of the diary, to make sure that I didn't miss any of Taylor's entries. Considering he had treated his diary as a kind of confidant, I was surprised that he simply stopped writing.

I wondered if, after the news about the death of Edgar, he became depressed, and whether that would explain it. I picked up my phone and looked at the list I had made of Taylor's compositions, and noted there was nothing listed between the end of 1914 and the beginning of 1917. Prior to 1914, however, he had been rather prolific. I knew that he hadn't served in the First World War, and so that was not the reason for the lack of compositions.

Going back to the diary, I found just two more entries for 1914.

August 10th,
And so we are at war.

War brings out a rather strange situation among the British: those who want to fight are told they cannot, and those who don't want to fight are the first to be made to do so.

I have been asked about my thoughts on the matter by the people of the village, as if being a composer makes me an expert on war. I detest war, and everything associated with it, but that is not a point of view which is popular at this point in time, and so I keep it to myself.

I can't help but think of Edgar, who would no doubt have been sent to fight. I wonder if, somehow, his life was better ended in the river he loved so much rather than fighting in a bloody war.

I miss him terribly. Sometimes, I even think that I see him, which is utter nonsense, of course. I dream of him often, and awaken to see him standing at the end of my bed, a remnant of the dream that fades within moments of me opening my eyes. I often wonder if I am to blame for his death. If I hadn't come home, would he even have been by the river on his own on that fateful day? I could perhaps have saved him if I had been there with him. I might not be able to swim, but I would have gladly given my life for his.

I have returned to work on the Festive Symphony, working on completing the orchestration. The best tribute I can think of for Edgar is to go ahead with the premiere later in the year as a form of tribute.

September 24th,
What have I done? I killed the beloved boy. I was so utterly selfish and stupid not to have realised it at the time, but now, in a letter from Mrs. Adams, the reality is laid out before me. I killed Edgar, just as I would have done if I had strangled him with my own hands. And that explains everything. It explains why I keep seeing him every time I start working on the third movement of the symphony – the movement that uses the melody that he taught me. I hear his voice all the while. I dream of him when I go to bed. The

symphony must never be performed. It must never be seen. That is the only way to rid myself of his presence, I am sure. My darling boy, I am so sorry.

I flicked through the rest of the diary, but Taylor had written no more. Was he really being haunted? Was *I* really being haunted? If so, was the key in that third movement? I was, after all, the first person to look at it in probably a hundred years. What if the playing of that melody that had been contributed by Edgar had... Had what? Brought him back? The idea seemed absurd.

I was about to close the diary, when I noticed that there was an envelope tucked inside at the back. I picked it up with trembling hands, and pulled out the letter that was inside.

20th September, 1914

Dear Mr. Taylor,

I have been unsure whether to write to you with the news that I received a few days ago, but I feel compelled to let you know the truth about what happened to Edgar. I know that you cared for him, and that he cared for you as well, albeit perhaps in a different way, I think. It seems only right that you know everything.

The inquest into Edgar's passing was opened and closed quickly. It was deemed an accident, and nothing more. That was several weeks ago, of course. And then, last week, I was visited by the village policeman. Another boy had come to see him, he said. It was one of the workers in the fields. He was very upset, saying that he couldn't keep what had happened to himself any longer, and he told the policeman everything.

Edgar had always been taunted by the other young men in the village, ever since he was a boy. Edgar had always denied it, but I knew it was true. Sensitive young men like my Edgar have always been singled out. Then, Mr. Taylor, the other young men had seen his friendship with you. One of them had seen you and Edgar on your last walk together. The policeman refused to tell me what had happened between you on that occasion, but I am not naïve, and can imagine for myself.

I know that, after that day, Edgar retreated into himself. He barely spoke to me – for days on end, sometimes. And this boy who had gone to the policeman told of how Edgar had been ostracised and tormented because of what had been seen. Edgar didn't drown by accident, Mr. Taylor. He was murdered. The policeman was told the full story by the boy that went to see him. He was down at the river with the others and they were pretending to be friendly with Edgar, and then one of them pounced on him and held his head under the water. It was supposed to be just a joke – a prank to scare him, but it went on for too long, and, eventually, Edgar stopped splashing around. He had drowned.

The boy who told all of this to the policeman said that all of them that were down at the river that day would swear that they had never gone, and that Edgar had been on his own, and drowned by accident. The young man that murdered Edgar has left the village, and nobody knows where he has gone – or so says this witness.

I realise that you didn't want any of this to happen, Mr. Taylor, and I want you to know that I do not hold you responsible for what happened to Edgar. However, I believe that you are the kind of man who would like to know the truth. I know that you meant him no harm, and that he enjoyed his time with you in those two weeks or so, just as you enjoyed your time with him. Bearing that in mind, I thought you might like to have a photograph of Edgar to remember him by, and enclose one with this letter.

I wish you all the best for the future, and hope for your sake that you do not have to get involved with this horrible war. At least Edgar has been spared that.
Yours sincerely,
Agatha Adams.

I reached into the envelope, and pulled out a small, somewhat faded, photograph. On the back was written the words "Edgar Henry Adams." As I turned over the photograph, I already knew that I would recognise the face I was going to be confronted with.

CHAPTER FIFTEEN

I put the letter and photograph back in the envelope and tucked it back inside the diary.

Henry was Edgar. I had known that something wasn't right about him, but I could never have guessed that he was…what? A ghost? I could think of no other word for it. Taylor had written about seeing Edgar every time he worked on the third movement after he had returned home, despite the fact that he thought at first his death was just an accident. And then he found out the truth. That would have been why the composer had destroyed his own work, and scrawled "WHAT HAVE I DONE?" at the top – the same words he used in his final diary entry of 1914. He had realised that it was his actions that had, inadvertently, resulted in Edgar's death.

And now, I had brought out the score of that symphony, which had been in a sealed envelope for a hundred years. I remembered again the lights flickering and the door rattling on that day when I had first set eyes on Taylor's work and, in particular, the destroyed manuscript for the third movement – the movement that featured Edgar's melody.

In short, by opening the sealed envelope, I had awakened Edgar's ghost. Perhaps it was simply the act of airing that possibly-ancient melody again that had summoned him. And I had fallen for him in much the same way that Taylor had. It seemed impossible, and yet it was true.

I felt a little stronger now that I understood what had been taking place over the previous month or so. The wet footprints in the hallway, the water in the bath, the running taps, the dead body I had momentarily seen in the bath. All of it led back to Edgar's drowning. But what was I to do about it now? Could I just put the music back into the envelope and seal it? That wouldn't be quite so easy. I had already told Frank about the discovery. Eventually he would want to see it. That was only natural. Well, if he wanted to see it, let him open the envelope himself next time.

I felt myself drawn to the window, and I walked over and looked down on the street below. The snow was coming down heavily, and it was clear from the lack of traffic going past that most people had decided to stay at home rather than brave the weather. But on the area just in front of the block of the flats was the same figure that I had seen there before, and, once again, he was looking up at my window.

It was Henry – or Edgar, as I now knew that he was. Just a few hours earlier, I would have run downstairs and brought him back up to my flat, where we would have…what? Made love, probably. But now I knew so much more. I had been talking with, and falling for, the ghost of a young man who had been murdered a hundred years ago. And he was outside, waiting for me.

The figure standing outside my block of flats terrified me, but I felt I should go down and confront it. It was the only way to end it, and so I grabbed my coat, put on some shoes, and slowly walked down the stairs to the ground floor. The lift never seemed to be working, but this time I was thankful for it.

My heart was racing as I reached the main door of the flats. I could see the figure ten metres or so away. For a few seconds, I just stared at it, not sure whether I wanted to confront it or run straight back to the relative safety of my own flat – or, perhaps, just leave Marlington completely, in the hope that I wouldn't be followed.

I slowly opened the door, the snow blowing straight into the building as I did so. The figure stared directly at me.

"What do you want?" I shouted, unwilling to move any closer to it.

There was no response, although I wasn't sure what kind of response I had expected. I stepped outside and took a few steps forward onto the pavement.

I could see now that the figure was soaked, it's hair matted over its eyes. The clothes were dripping wet, but the water made no effect on the snow-covered path beneath.

"What do you want?" I repeated, and watched in terror as the ghost of Edgar started moving towards me.

I lost my nerve. I went back into the flats, and ran up the first flight of stairs before turning around. The figure was inside now, at the bottom of the stairs. I wasn't going to wait to see what would happen next, and continued up the rest of the stairs to my own flat, shutting the door behind me and locking it – as if I thought that would keep out what was coming for me.

I moved down the hallway, not sure of what to do next, but heard a strange sound coming from behind me. I turned around to see water emerging from under the front door of my flat. It had to have been coming from the main stairwell, but I was certain that nobody standing out there would have been able to see it. I watched the water continue to enter the flat from under the door, and then it started to rise up from the floor, taking the shape of the ghost of Edgar that I had seen outside.

I didn't know what to do. It clearly wanted me, and I had no idea how to stop it. I could only assume that my unsealing of the envelope that contained the symphony made it associate me with Taylor himself. It blamed me – or, perhaps, the symphony itself – for its death. Probably the latter. That melody he had contributed had summoned it.

The figure was complete now. It stood there in front of the door, arms outstretched, reaching for me. Trying to claim me, I thought, in the same way that the river had claimed *it*. And, as it stood there, I heard the taps in the kitchen and bathroom turn on, and the more the water ran, the more strength the figure in front of me seemed to get.

I backed down the hallway as it came towards me, moving into the living room, where the score for the symphony and the diaries were. I was still wondering whether it had come for them or for me. As the ghost entered the living room, I picked up the score for the symphony, and held it out in front of me.

"Is this what you want?" I yelled at it. "Do you want this, so that nobody will ever get to hear it?"

It stopped moving. Perhaps that really was the answer – that it wanted the symphony.

I held out the papers in front of me, and edged forward, thinking the ghost might somehow reach out and grab them from me. I was close enough to touch it with the manuscript now, and, as I thrusted the papers at it, it made a screeching sound that was utterly horrifying. I cowered on the floor in fear, thinking it might at least bring my neighbours to my flat to see what the commotion was about, and then realised that it was probably only I who heard it. They wouldn't have seen the figure either, when it was standing outside.

If it didn't want the manuscript, the only other

option was that it wanted me to destroy it. I backed up across the room and grabbed the matches that I had left on a shelf when I had lighted the Christmas candles prior to Carla arriving that afternoon. As I struck a match, the figure started moving towards me once again. The flame went out before I could even touch the papers with it. My hands were shaking too much with fear.

I tried for a second time, my hands still trembling, knowing that I only had a few seconds before the figure reached me. This time, the match touched the score of the symphony and the papers started to burn.

I threw them into the wastepaper bin, and watched as the flames consumed them, and the figure in front of me paused, and then started backing away, slowly moving out of the living room and then retreating down the hall, and finally returning to water and escaping under the door of my flat, in much the same manner as I had seen it come in just a few minutes earlier.

When it had gone, the smoke alarms started to sound, and I took the bin of burning papers (or what was left of them) and held them under the running tap in the bath, before opening all of the windows in the flat, and flapping papers around the smoke alarm until it switched off.

CHAPTER SIXTEEN

I was horrified by what I had seen, read and done.

The symphony that Alfred Taylor had sealed in an envelope over a century earlier had gone, this time for good. There would be no first performance of what was undoubtedly the composer's greatest work, and I realised that was exactly how it had to be. It filled me with sadness, having had to destroy the score. But what had been my other option? Falling prey to a ghost?

I didn't tell Frank what had happened to the score – which he had told me not to take home. I could have told a version of the truth, that the photocopier hadn't been working, and so I had taken the original papers home and there had been a tragic accident. He probably would have accepted my explanation, but I no longer had any interest in my research or the Taylor papers. They could *all* go up in smoke for all I cared.

THE FESTIVE SYMPHONY

By the new year, I had left Marlington. I had sent an email to the university stating that I was withdrawing from the PhD. Frank sent me a reply, trying to find out what had happened, but I ignored it, and then blocked his email address. I sent the diary back to the university with no note or explanation, and assumed that it found its way back to the rest of the Taylor paraphernalia.

Just after I returned to the insurance company that I had been working at prior to starting the PhD, I spoke to Clara and told her everything. I have no idea whether she believed me or not. I have a suspicion that she simply thought I needed to see a doctor, and that my mental health problems had returned. But that wouldn't explain why I rarely heard from her afterwards. If she thought that I was ill, I would have expected her to be in contact with me more, not less. There was one or two comments from her on the few posts I made on Facebook in the year that followed, but little else, and, the following Christmas, I didn't receive a card.

Had she finally given up on our friendship, that she had tried so hard over the years to continue? No, I didn't think so. It was much more likely that she knew that, without her intervention, I would never have attended the wedding, and none of the events I have just documented would have happened.

THE END

Read on for an exclusive extract from *Welcome to Marlington*, the first novel in *The Marlington Chronicles.*

OVERTURE

The city of Marlington, situated around thirty miles from the English east coast, has a reputation of being one of the most picturesque cities in the country, and that reputation is well-earned. There are more trees and green spaces than in any other town or city in England. This fact is proudly displayed on all of the signs at the city's borders, below the words "Welcome to Marlington." It is one of the few places where one can come out of the main indoor shopping mall and be able to enter a park after a walk of less than one hundred metres. To add to this, it has more than its fair share of historic buildings and sites of interest, from the Roman city wall through to numerous houses and pubs that date back up to seven hundred years. It is no surprise that it remains a popular tourist destination.

Marlington Castle sits on a man-made mound in the centre of the city. The imposing Norman structure looks down from its vantage point, as if keeping a watchful eye on the people below as they go about their daily business. The building has had a varied

WELCOME TO MARLINGTON (EXTRACT)

history, starting off as a royal palace before becoming the county gaol in the 15th century. During its four hundred years as a prison, it housed some of the most infamous criminals of the time, and was the site of many hangings, some of which were watched by crowds in their tens of thousands. But that was a long time ago. For the last one hundred years it has been home to the city library, with a significant special collection of local interest books, papers and artefacts that has attracted researchers and scholars not only from across the region, but also from across the country – and even the world. Some of the books housed there date back over seven hundred years, and the library prides itself on having the facilities to keep such priceless items in an archive room with perfect storage conditions.

Directly below the castle is the main shopping district of the city, much of which was rebuilt after World War II due to the damage caused by air raids. Some of the most popular stores of the time had their premises destroyed on a single night in 1942 when the bombings led to a fire that spread quickly down the main high street and into the centuries-old marketplace. Temporary accommodation was found for some of them, and one department store set up a makeshift shop in a number of double-decker buses in the store's car park while it waited to find a new home. Marlington suffered more during the war than many other cities in the same part of the country. Over two thousand homes were destroyed, and the civilian

WELCOME TO MARLINGTON (EXTRACT)

casualties reached almost five hundred. But, by this point in its history, Marlington was quite used to disaster.

Below the shopping area of the city are a warren of so-called underground streets that were rediscovered relatively recently. These were originally not underground at all, but were built over in the late 1800s with the shops and other buildings that are now at street level, when an effort was made to fill in the defensive ditches that surrounded the castle. There are also rumours of a maze of underground tunnels running under the entire city, some of which are said to lead directly to the dungeons of the castle. None of these have yet been found, but neither have the funds needed to search for them. Perhaps one day they will give up their secrets.

A relatively short walk north from the shopping centre will bring you to the city's cathedral. It is an imposing building with gothic architecture, built in the late 1800s following a fire on May 8th, 1864, that caused so much damage to the Norman cathedral that had stood there for eight centuries that the structure as a whole became unsafe and had to be demolished. Much of the stone from the first cathedral was re-used in the second, and the few stained-glass windows that survived the blaze were also transferred to the new building. The cause of the fire remains a mystery, but it claimed several hundred lives after taking hold during a service on that fateful Sunday morning, and it remains unclear as to why the congregation at the

WELCOME TO MARLINGTON (EXTRACT)

service couldn't get out before the fire had spread.

Many local residents still believe that May 8th is an unlucky day, not just because it was the date of the cathedral disaster, but also because the 1942 air raid that resulted in the major fire on the high street also took place on the same day. One local researcher, Cecilia master's, even spent several weeks in the special collection in the library in the 1950s, looking back at May 8th through the centuries in the hope of rubbishing the idea that the day was an unlucky one for the city. However, she found that there were many more murders, accidents, and riots in Marlington and the surrounding area on that day of the year than on any other. Miss master's' work was not published until eight years after she committed suicide (on May 8th, 1963), at which point it was sent anonymously to the local newspaper. The newspaper was heavily criticised by some readers at the time for making the information public, with many stating that they thought the publication was giving column inches to nothing more than a set of morbid coincidences. Coincidences or not, Cecilia master's' findings were uncomfortable reading.

To the east of the city is a large area made up of woodland and heathland, which has also seen much bloodshed through the centuries. Back in the 13th century, it was the site of a particularly heinous murder, the news of which spread far and wide across the country, and made the city of Marlington famous for all the wrong reasons. A book was written not long

WELCOME TO MARLINGTON (EXTRACT)

after the murder, accusing a small community living on the outskirts of the city of committing the crime. Despite the accusations not being true (and motivated by pure religious hatred), a large group from Marlington went after them for revenge, burning down their houses one night, and killing more than thirty people.

During the English Civil War, the same area was the site of the infamous Battle of Marlington Heath, fought between the royalists of the city and a force of parliamentarians. It is said that over three thousand people perished during those three days, and this is reflected in the change in population figures for the city during the same period. Today, this is a popular site for picnickers, walkers, and cyclists, but there are regular reports of unusual sounds and manifestations. While some have ultimately been explained away, there are several photographs and, increasingly, video footage that have yet to find a logical explanation. These have been discussed endlessly on internet sites, and some have even made it into the national tabloid press. Attempts were made by a popular ghost-hunting television show to film in the area in order to investigate the apparently-supernatural events, but their equipment failed them each time they tried to film.

It is fair to say that Marlington has more than its fair share of hauntings and local myths and mysteries, and the so-called ghosts of Marlington Heath are only a small part of that. Many visitors to the Castle Library

WELCOME TO MARLINGTON (EXTRACT)

have reported seeing strange apparitions, particularly on one of the main staircases and, perhaps more unnervingly, in the lift, where a hangman's noose is sometimes seen, suspended in mid-air, when the doors open. The sound of rattling chains and banging doors have been heard by those who work in the library during the day, and by the security guards at night. Elsewhere, ghostly monks have been seen in St Cecilia's Hall, a concert venue that incorporates the remains of an old monastery. Also, a spectral dog-like creature with large teeth and a foaming mouth has been seen in a number of sites around the city, including in some of the parks and wooded areas. Most people assume it is just a wild animal, but not everyone is convinced.

Perhaps most unusual for an English city in the 21st century is the legend of the "drager," a term that appears to derive from the Norse word "draugr," used to describe a type of demon or undead creature. The Marlington dragers are said to be vampire-like creatures that don't feed on human blood, but on death and misery itself. Local folklore tells us that these creatures feed sporadically by, for example, causing disasters with a significant loss of life, and they then live among us unnoticed. However, over time, they are said to grow weaker and have to retreat from society as their physical appearance changes, having to bide their time until they have no strength left, and it is only at that point that they can then feed again. There are still people in Marlington and the surrounding villages

WELCOME TO MARLINGTON (EXTRACT)

that believe these stories, probably due to the local history of fire, battles, murder, and plague.

One can perhaps appreciate just how seriously the myth of the drager has been taken in this part of the country when you travel to the west of the city centre, where there are roads named "Drager Avenue" and "Drager Way." These are situated in the area of Marlington now dominated by student housing, where landlords have bought up most of the terraced housing near the university, and rent it to students at inflated prices. The average three-bedroomed house with lounge and dining room is generally rented out as a five-bedroom property, so that more income can be generated. Perhaps the names of Drager Avenue and Drager Way are apt in an area where students' bank balances are bled dry by vampiric landlords.

We can't end our little tour of Marlington without mentioning the river that flows through the city. The River Marl connects the city to the North Sea some thirty miles away. At one time it carried a great deal of commercial traffic to and from Marlington. The river has been the subject of many landscape paintings, especially at the point where it runs alongside the grounds of the cathedral, a particularly beautiful spot where many holiday makers now like to moor their boat for a night or two when they spend a week cruising the network of waterways in the area. There is also a public footpath following the river as it winds its way from the east of the city to the west. Even this is said to be haunted by a woman who jumped in the

WELCOME TO MARLINGTON (EXTRACT)

river when committing suicide.

But, for now, we must return to the shopping area. On a side street, not far from the newly-renovated bus station, is a large building built in the late 18th century that has been the home of the famous Marlington Insurance Company for close to two hundred years. It is the workplace for hundreds of city residents and often for students who temp there part-time so that they can get a little extra cash to keep them afloat.

So, let us make our way through those famous revolving doors that have appeared on so many television commercials for the company, walk through the foyer, get in the lift, and press the button for the fourth floor. When we exit the lift, we need to take the corridor to the left, which leads us straight into a large open-plan office area where close to fifty workers sit at their computers, inputting data or talking to customers (or potential customers) on the telephone. On the far wall is a tea and coffee machine and a vending machine containing chocolate, crisps and protein bars – after all, workers getting their fill of caffeine and sugar have more short-term energy than those without. Above the machines is a giant clock, which many of those in the office watch from the moment they arrive in the morning until the moment they leave at night.

In the centre of the office space, a middle-aged man sits at a computer. His name is Aaron Melton, and it is his untimely demise that begins our story.

WELCOME TO MARLINGTON (EXTRACT)

ONE

The clock on the computer changed from 16:59 to 17:00. At that precise moment, the unlikely named Aaron Madison Melton took one of the Marks and Spencer mints from the little green tin on his desk and popped it inside his mouth, lodging it between his teeth and his cheek with a little help from his tongue.

This was the ninth and last mint that he would have while at work that day. He repeated this small but precise routine every hour, on the hour, during each working day. He wasn't quite sure what the repercussions would be if he didn't do this, but he didn't want to find out either. He knew that many people with obsessive compulsive disorder thought harm might come to their families if they didn't carry out their self-assigned tasks with precision, but Aaron Madison Melton did not have this precise fear.

He didn't have much family to speak of anyway, other than Judy, his sister – and he couldn't remember the last time he had seen her. She had made a concerted effort to *not* see Aaron for some years. Perhaps the last time they had met had been at their brother's funeral. He had thrown himself in the River Marl without warning one day eight years earlier. Or was it seven? Aaron wasn't very good with dates. His brother hadn't died in the river, however, and so had thrown himself in front of a train a week later. Judy had blamed Aaron. After all, he lived in the same city as his brother and so, in her mind, should have been able to stop the tragedy. The fact that waiting lists for mental health treatments made it impossible for her brother to get treatment after his first suicide attempt was something that hadn't crossed Judy's mind.

So, no, Aaron wasn't concerned about a family tragedy occurring if he didn't keep to his mint schedule. He just knew *something* bad would happen. No-one, including himself, knew why the mint routine was only a requirement between 9.00 and 5.00 each day, and little progress had been made in attempts to break with the routine. He wasn't that worried; he knew people with considerably more disabling OCD habits than sucking on mints and was glad that he did not have to deal with them.

Aaron logged off from the computer in front of him and then pushed back his chair, stood up, and put on his jacket. It had seen better days. The pockets had holes in them, and there was a small rip in the back. It could do with a wash, too, but that would mean wearing a different jacket for a couple of days, and Aaron didn't like the idea of that very much. He liked this one and he felt comfortable in it, rain or shine.

Various goodbyes were muttered to Aaron as he picked up his large umbrella and walked out of the office.

Despite his often-peculiar ways, he wasn't disliked by his work colleagues at the Marlington Insurance Company. He was, perhaps, viewed as something of a "character," but he kept himself to himself and he did his work as required each day, and hadn't had a day off

WELCOME TO MARLINGTON (EXTRACT)

sick in six-and-a-half years. Aaron was reliable; there was no doubt about that. Jokes were made about him behind his back, but they were good-natured – or as good-natured as jokes made behind backs can be. A boy who came to the office once as part of his school work experience commented to one of the workers that Aaron looked and acted a bit like a stereotypical serial killer. It was unlikely that many disagreed with him but, all the same, the boy was barely spoken to by anyone in the office for the rest of his time there. They did not like people speaking badly of Aaron.

Aaron waited for the lift and then made his way down four floors before going outside and starting on his walk home, using the golfing umbrella as if it were a walking cane.

Aaron hated his name. There were lots of things about himself he could hate. He was no stunner when it came to the looks department, that was for sure, although he was proud of himself for losing three stones in weight over the last eighteen months. And he certainly could hate himself for having remained single for all of his forty-eight years, only ever having been kissed when someone was dared to do it just before he left school. It went without saying that Aaron was a virgin. He had thought at one point about paying for sex in order to experience it at least once in his life. However, deep down, the idea of sex rather revolted him, and he was certain that he would be useless at it anyway. Bearing that in mind, he used the money to go to the theatre instead. Aaron liked the

WELCOME TO MARLINGTON (EXTRACT)

theatre, especially when it was half empty, and he didn't have to sit close to anyone else.

Despite his bachelor status, his looks, and his non-existent sex life, it was still his name he hated most. It didn't suit him; it didn't feel like *his*. What's more, his name was a constant reminder to him of his parents having sex.

His parents had travelled to New York in June 1972 in order to see Elvis Presley perform at Madison Square Garden. After the concert that evening, Marjorie and Graham Melton returned to their hotel room and Aaron was the end result. Aaron had been named after the person the newspapers that week had called a "prince from another planet," and the place in which his parents had seen him perform. Aaron often felt like *he* was from another planet. To make things worse, his parents had owned the album of the concert they had seen and which was indirectly responsible for Aaron, and had often played it, reminding him that, if it wasn't for that concert, he might not be there at all. When he was fourteen, he brought a school friend back to the house (his only school friend, as it happened). His parents played the album for him too, telling him the full story that went with it. The boy never came back, and barely spoke to Aaron afterwards.

Despite his rather unorthodox upbringing, Aaron grew up relatively "well-adjusted". That was the term his counsellor used, anyway. Aaron preferred the blunter "normal". He had been a loner, yes, but he had always liked his own company, and so that didn't

WELCOME TO MARLINGTON (EXTRACT)

bother him. And he had gone to university, too, even gaining a doctorate.

It had been ten years ago, just after his thirty-eighth birthday, that a traumatic event occurred from which Aaron had never quite recovered. He had seen a young homeless man being attacked in the park, and had failed to chase off the attackers, with the man dying in Aaron's arms while he waited for the ambulance to arrive. His co-workers knew the basic story which had been passed from colleague to colleague over the years, and that, in part, was the reason why Aaron was accepted by those around him, despite the fact he had what his sister called "issues."

He whistled as he walked down the street. *Not* Elvis, it should be said. He had never shared his parent's passion for the King of Rock 'n' Roll. Perhaps that Madison Square Garden album had been played too often when he was a child. No, light opera was more Aaron's bag, and today his song of choice was *When the Night Wind Howls* from *Ruddigore*. He wasn't quite sure where he had dredged the song up from, and had not listened to Gilbert and Sullivan in quite some time – not since he was at the local G & S society and mistakenly thought a new member was flirting with him. It turned out that wasn't the case and Aaron was too embarrassed to ever return.

He missed the yearly productions, and he liked to think that they missed him too. He thought that he could certainly hold a tune, and had an excellent memory for the lyrics of the patter songs. He was

WELCOME TO MARLINGTON (EXTRACT)

certain that his turns as John Wellington Wells and the Modern Major-General in *The Sorcerer* and *The Pirates of Penzance* respectively were the highlights of those shows. Not all of those who had seen the productions thought the same.

As was his custom (and he *was* a man of habit), Aaron took a slight detour down St. William's Street so that he could make a stop at Gregg's. The temptation was too much.

He looked with some dismay at the number of empty buildings on what was traditionally Marlington's busiest shopping street. Some had been empty for a long time, like the massive shop that had been British Home Stores until 2016. It had been used for a while as a temporary home for Next while they performed building works at their own store, but now it was eerily deserted. Other shops had shut their doors during Coronavirus lockdowns and never re-opened. The old Argos store was a case in point. A couple of years earlier, it had still been one of the busiest shops during the Christmas period, and now it wasn't open at all. Each time Aaron passed the empty shops on the way home from work, he wondered why good use couldn't be made of the empty buildings. There were people sleeping on the streets, and yet there were huge unused spaces like these which were left deserted. Aaron often thought about people who lived on the streets.

When he came out of Gregg's (Aaron was very pleased that *they* had reopened after lockdown), he had

WELCOME TO MARLINGTON (EXTRACT)

a small loaf of freshly baked bread in his bag and a hot sausage roll in his hand that he ate in a way that made him considerably less attractive than he already was. By the time he reached the underpass, the only visible evidence that there had ever been a sausage roll at all were the small remnants of flaky pastry that inadvertently clung to his lips. He wiped at his mouth and walked through the underpass quickly, heading towards Finch Gardens, a park that would cut around ten minutes off his journey if he walked through it.

He started his walk through the park. There were relatively few people there, with it still being mid-February and there being a particularly biting east wind. Snow had been forecast for the weekend, something that Aaron was not looking forward to. The kids on his road were not to be trusted in such weather. He laughed when they threw snowballs at him, but hated every moment of it. During the most recent snowfall, Aaron had awoken to the sight of a snowman with a giant penis in his front garden. While many would have found it amusing, Aaron found it distasteful.

Aaron smiled broadly at a man coming towards him who was walking his cocker spaniel. He smiled at the dog, too. The man didn't smile back; even the dog didn't take any notice of him. Aaron shrugged his shoulders with indifference and continued his walk through the park.

He wasn't sure at what point he first heard the noise, but he had become aware of shouting coming

WELCOME TO MARLINGTON (EXTRACT)

from the far side of the park. He looked across and saw a group of teenage boys who he assumed were playing a game of some kind. Probably football. A bit cold for such things, Aaron thought, but kids seemed to be immune to the temperature.

He continued walking, but as he did so he felt a growing sense of unease about the boys. If they were playing football, he couldn't see a ball or any makeshift goal. What he *could* see was another boy on the ground, in a foetal position with his hands covering his head. He stopped and watched, and saw that the boy was being beaten by the others. He was just lying still on the floor while they kicked and spat at him, and yelled obscenities.

Aaron wasn't quite sure what he should do, but knew that he had to do something. Memories came flooding back to him of the incident ten years earlier. He wasn't about to let this boy die in the way that the homeless man had. Instinctively, he left the footpath and walked quickly across the grass to the boys. He held his umbrella out in front of him and found himself shouting, "Oi, you! Leave that lad alone!" He had no idea where or how he had found the nerve to shout at the boys; it was quite an achievement for someone who kept to himself so much. However, his words didn't seem to make any impact, and the beating of the boy on the ground continued.

Aaron picked up his pace, and shouted again. This time, the boys stopped and looked at him.

"Leave that boy alone!" he shouted at them for a

second time.

"Piss off!" one of the attackers shouted back.

"I will call the police!" Aaron said. "I have my mobile phone. Look!"

Aaron was still extremely proud of the fact that he had finally entered the new millennium and obtained a small mobile phone. He had done so some twenty years later than most people, but it was a milestone for him.

The boys left their victim curled up on the ground and walked over to Aaron. The leader got up close to him, grabbed the mobile phone from his hand, threw it down on the ground, and stamped his foot on it repeatedly.

"I told you to piss off," the boy spat in Aaron's face.

"I want…want the name and address of your parents," Aaron stammered, rather shocked at his own bravery. "They will have to pay for the damage to my mobile phone."

"Oh, will they?" the boy responded, before punching Aaron, first in the face, and then again in his stomach.

Aaron was not in a physical state to be able to defend himself, despite the weight loss that he was very proud of. He collapsed to his knees, and his umbrella fell on the ground beside him.

At that moment, another boy came forward and kicked him in the face, which resulted in Aaron lying flat on his back on the cold, wet grass. Unlike the boy whose beating Aaron had tried to stop, he was not savvy enough to try to shield himself from the punches and kicks that followed. They probably only lasted for a couple of minutes, but it seemed like hours to Aaron before he lost consciousness while wondering why no-one had come to try to intervene.

By that point, Aaron's face was a bloody mess, and several of his ribs were broken. What ultimately killed him, however, was when the leader of the gang picked up Aaron's umbrella and drove it repeatedly into his stomach.

Aaron lay still on the ground, the life draining from his body. Nobody had run over to help him. Nobody had called the police. Nobody in the park that day had dared to; they didn't have the same bravery that Aaron exhibited when he went to the aid of the young boy who he had seen being beaten.

The teenagers looked down upon the lifeless body, almost as if they were unable to comprehend quite what had happened. After a few seconds, the leader took a small black book from his pocket, placed it carefully on the ground beside Aaron's body, and then he and his friends walked off.

Welcome to Marlington is available from Amazon and selected other online bookstores.

Printed in Great Britain
by Amazon